INSPECTOR WEST REGRETS

CONDITIONS OF SALE

JOHN CREASEY

INSPECTOR WEST
REGRETS

UNABRIDGED

PAN BOOKS LTD · LONDON

First published 1945 by Stanley Paul Ltd.
First revised edition published 1965 by
Hodder and Stoughton Ltd.
This edition published 1970 by Pan Books Ltd,
33 Tothill Street, London, S.W.1

ISBN 0 330 02588 0

*The characters in this story are entirely
imaginary and bear no relation to any living person*

*Made and Printed in Great Britain by
Cox & Wyman Ltd, London, Reading, and Fakenham*

CHAPTER ONE

Roger West in Ecstasy

CHIEF INSPECTOR ROGER WEST of New Scotland Yard was talking to his wife on the telephone. He sat in his office, which he shared with four other detectives of equal rank. On his handsome face – he was so good-looking that most of his friends called him 'Handsome' – was a fatuous smile. From time to time he burst out with an incredulous exclamation, such as:

'*No!*' or '*You'd never believe it!*' or '*Astonishing!*' and gave a little laugh. Over a period of three months his fellow inspectors had grown used to these remarkable manifestations of delight. Usually as soon as Janet West came through they made their way out of the office, leaving Roger to his ecstasy. Except Eddie Day; no one ever expected Eddie Day to show tact. Eddie was a man of medium height, running to fat, with prominent teeth and a weak chin. He was a specialist on forgery. There were marked deficiencies in his mental make-up, but in his particular sphere he was unchallenged.

Eddie was examining some letters. If they were forgeries then the police would be able to prosecute a gentleman suspected of writing extremely clever begging letters. Eddie breathed heavily and noisily through his mouth as he concentrated.

On the instant that the door opened, he shot one startled, nervous look towards Roger West, straightened up, and let a watch-glass fall from his eye. Then he pushed back his chair and stood up, saying in a loud voice:

'*Good* morning, *sir!*'

' 'Morning, Day,' said Sir Guy Chatworth, the Assistant Commissioner.

'I haven't got my report quite ready yet, sir,' gabbled

5

Eddie. 'Another couple of hours should see me through, though.'

'That's all right,' said Chatworth. 'I came to see West.'

Roger suddenly leaned forward, doubled up with laughter, and cried:

'*Never!*'

Chatworth moved forward, and stood just behind Roger, who had no idea of his presence.

'*Marvellous!*' he exclaimed. 'And only four months! Oh, the other one won't be long. They *always* come in pairs, I'm told.'

'And we haven't had *any* trouble,' said his wife, and went on: 'But darling, are you busy?'

'Not the slightest bit,' said Roger, 'it's the slackest morning I've had for months. Eddie Day has just scuttled out of the office. What was that?'

As Janet went into further details about the subject under discussion, Roger's elbow slipped off the desk. He saw Chatworth's sand-coloured waistcoat across which stretched a black leather watch-strap. Both were vaguely familiar. He looked down, to see a pair of baggy plus fours and highly polished brown shoes. He looked up, to see a red neck, a round, red face and a fringe of curly grey hair around a pink, bald cranium.

To his everlasting credit, he kept his voice steady.

'That's marvellous, darling, but I must go now, I think the AC wants to see me. . . . What? . . . Yes, I certainly will tell him. Goodbye!'

He replaced the receiver, straightened up, and looked at Chatworth with a tentative smile.

'Good morning, sir.'

'Good morning, Inspector West,' said Chatworth, his deep voice loaded with dangerous courtesy. 'I must apologize for disturbing you. May I be so bold as to inquire what you will certainly tell me?'

'Pass on my wife's regards, sir. She asked me to tell you that your godson is doing splendidly.'

For a fleeting moment the suspicion of a twinkle showed in Chatworth's blue eyes.

'I am very glad to hear it, but less pleased to hear that you have so little to do, Inspector.'

'That was just to reassure Janet,' said Roger, and added appealingly: 'I only see the infant for half an hour in the mornings, sir. He's just over twelve pounds, and so fat that he can hardly see out of his eyes! And happy! You—' He stopped himself.

'Whether I was wise to let myself in for being his god-father I don't know,' Chatworth said. 'If he grows up anything like his father he will have the nerve of Old Harry! Without necessarily referring to the discussion you've just had, you are not overloaded with work, are you?'

'I'm just clearing up the Galloway case,' said Roger. 'As a matter of fact, sir, I've been wondering if I can take a long weekend.'

'In which to gambol with the infant prodigy,' said Chatworth. 'If nothing develops I don't see why not.' He put a letter which he was holding on to Roger's desk. 'I think we'll have to see what we can find out about this.'

'Another one, sir?' exclaimed Roger, glancing at the letter.

'We've now had five in five days. This fellow is being very persistent, and he might know what he's talking about.'

Roger took the letter and read it quickly. It was type-written, had no address and no signature, and said:

You'd better not wait much longer before you see what K. is up to. You'll be sorry if you don't take my tip.

The 'K' in the letter referred to Mr Andrew Kelham. Kelham was a well-known financier whose activities had long been suspect, and the police had watched him closely, as well as investigated many of his undertakings. He was a plausible, amiable and good-looking man of middle-age who was busy financing private schemes for estate development in greater London and provincial towns. There was nothing wrong in that. The earlier letters, however, had declared that he was planning to evade regulations. There was great scope for such evasion in land values.

Roger flicked the letter with his forefinger.

'I hardly know where to start, sir.'

'You'd better get the file out and go through it. It shouldn't stop you from having your weekend. I'll send the other letters along to you. I won't expect miracles at first.' He nodded, and went out, but as Roger glanced at the letter again, he opened the door and said: 'Oh, West.'

Roger looked up.

'What come in pairs?' asked Chatworth.

'Pairs?' echoed Roger, puzzled.

'You said something on the telephone about "they always come in pairs",' said Chatworth. 'I warn you, West, you'll have to look elsewhere for a godfather if—'

Roger hooted. 'I meant teeth; he's got one in the upper jaw. The incisors usually come in pairs, according to all the best books! When children come in pairs they're usually known as twins.'

'Are they indeed?' Chatworth went out.

Roger was grinning when Eddie Day came in, obviously having watched the door.

'I tried to warn you, Handsome,' he said. 'I've told you before that you'll get into trouble if you don't take more notice of the AC. Did you get it hot and strong?' He seemed hopeful.

'He was quite amiable,' said Roger.

Eddie shook his head, sadly.

'I don't know how you do it,' he admitted. 'I just don't know, Handsome. If he caught me wasting my time on the telephone like that I'd never hear the last of it. And I've got *five*.'

'What, teeth?'

'No, kids. What on earth made you say "teeth"?'

A messenger from Chatworth came in with the other anonymous letters. Roger sent the same man to get the file on Andrew Kelham, and took the papers with him when he went to lunch. He spent the whole afternoon sifting through the various items of information, but could find nothing new. All there had been against Kelham were vague suspicions and the fact that he had been known to associate with convicted operators in land speculation –

8

two of whom had received big payments against forged documents and land titles. It occurred to Roger to make a list of all the men who had been convicted of such offences and had been acquainted with Kelham: the total was seventeen.

He telephoned Inspector Sloan, who on his recommendation had recently been promoted, and passed on this piece of information. Sloan spoke thoughtfully.

'I suppose if you tried, you'd find other men with as many crooked contacts, and yet with their hands quite clean.'

'I wonder if I would. It's an impressive list. I don't like the feeling that Kelham may be sitting back and laughing at us.'

'What are you going to do?'

'I can't make up my mind,' said Roger. 'It's no use bursting in on the man and plying him with questions, and I don't fancy the idea of tackling his staff again.'

'Did the AC say why he'd decided to take it seriously?'

'No, he didn't. Bill, will you come to Chelsea this evening? I'll take the papers home with me. We may see something if we put our heads together.'

'I'll be glad to,' Sloan said.

'Good man,' said Roger. 'Make it seven o'clock, the infant will be in bed by then.' He rang off, and after some minutes of contemplation, telephoned Janet. When she answered him Roger could hear in the background the cries of the infant Martin.

'Would it be too great a strain if Bill Sloan and Mark Lessing come to supper?' Roger asked.

'No, I'll manage,' said Janet. 'I must fly, darling, he's yelling his head off.'

Roger put through another call, this time to Mark Lessing, a close personal friend with an inquiring mind. Mark promised to be at Roger's Chelsea house before half past seven. It was then six o'clock.

Roger would have left immediately afterwards but for a troubled sergeant who wanted some information about the Galloway case, and it was a quarter to seven before he locked his desk and was ready to leave. All the others had gone. Outside, the evening was dull after a typical April day with heavy rain interspersed with bright sunshine, and the windows showed yellow squares of light against the gloom. He put on his raincoat and hat and went downstairs, but he was only halfway down the steps leading to the courtyard on the Embankment side when he was called:

'Handsome!'

He looked round, and saw a fellow inspector.

'Aren't you on the K business?' called the inspector.

'Yes, why?' asked Roger.

'Kelham's son's been murdered,' the inspector said. 'You'd better go, hadn't you?'

CHAPTER TWO

The Murder of Anthony Kelham

IT was nearly dark when Roger reached Kelham's Park Lane flat with a sergeant and two detective officers. The block of luxury flats was glowing with subdued wall-lighting. A uniformed porter led the party to the second floor.

Roger knew that Kelham's son was a youth of twenty-one, who had been sent down from Oxford after a few months, for throwing parties described as 'orgiastic'; his sexual morals had a farmyard complex, the police had discovered. At that time he was more than usually sensitive about fathers and sons and was quite prepared to be sympathetic with Andrew Kelham.

A sleek, well-dressed man opened the door; Blair, Kelham's private secretary.

'Inspector West, isn't it? I'm glad you've arrived so quickly. Mr Kelham is very much upset.'

'Naturally,' said Roger.

'I know you'll excuse my indiscretion,' Blair said, 'but if you can go easy on questions, I'm sure he would be grateful.'

'I won't make it any worse than I must,' Roger said.

'That's very good of you,' said Blair.

He was a curiously self-effacing individual. In the course of his earlier inquiries Roger had come across him several times, and always come away with the impression that he was a perfect secretary.

'I'll tell him you've arrived,' he said.

'Before you do that, tell me what happened,' said Roger. His men put their cases down, and one began to stand a camera on a tripod. The large sitting-room into which they had been led was expensively and tastefully furnished. The flat was very quiet.

'I'm afraid I can't tell you much,' said Blair. 'Tony – that is, Anthony Kelham – was in his father's library, sitting at the desk. Mr Kelham and I had been out for the afternoon. When we came back Tony was sitting at the desk. I think you will find that he had been shot in the back.'

'Have you moved him?'

'No.'

'Have you touched anything in the room?'

'Nothing at all has been disturbed,' Blair said.

'Had Anthony Kelham any right to be in the library?'

'Every right. No part of the flat was locked against him.' Blair hesitated. 'Isn't that rather a curious question, Inspector?'

Roger ignored that.

'What time did you get back?'

'A little after half past six.'

'It's now twenty past seven,' said Roger, and thought of the little gathering at Chelsea. 'May we use your telephone?'

'It's in that corner,' said Blair.

'Thanks. Willis, telephone Mrs West for me, will you, and tell her that I have been delayed and probably won't be home until late.' He turned back to Blair. 'What time did Anthony Kelham arrive?'

'He was due here at five o'clock,' said Blair.

'What do the servants say?'

'No one was on duty. There is only a woman and her daughter, both dailies. We have our meals in the restaurant.' Blair lit a cigarette. 'I'm afraid I can't be more precise about the time that Tony reached here, Inspector, and I assure you that Mr Kelham can't.'

'I see,' said Roger, and turned to a sergeant. 'Go downstairs and find out whether the commissionaire or anyone else saw Mr Anthony Kelham come in this evening.' When the man had gone, he added to Blair: 'I'm very glad you lost no time; that should be helpful. You've no theories, I suppose?'

'I've never been so astonished,' said Blair. 'Hadn't you better see Mr Kelham?'

'Is he alone?'

'Yes,' said Blair. 'Mrs Kelham is away.'

Roger nodded, and Blair went into the hall ahead of him and tapped at one of the five doors leading from it.

A hoarse voice called 'come in'. As Roger entered the room, Andrew Kelham was sitting at a bureau desk, reading something in front of him, and his attitude was one of utter dejection. Roger, remembering a man of immaculate attire, tall, well groomed and with admirable poise, had a fleeting impression that Kelham looked years older.

'What is it, Blair?' Kelham asked, without looking round.

'Inspector West, of New Scotland Yard.'

'Ah, yes, of course,' said Kelham.

The impression of age was strengthened when he stood up and turned to face Roger. Usually he was smiling; now his expression was one of mute despair. He still held the letter. His collar was crumpled, his hair dishevelled; single hairs were on his collar and shoulders.

'I'm glad you've come, Inspector. Blair has told you what – what happened?'

'I'm very sorry to hear of it,' said Roger. 'I won't worry you now more than I must, Mr Kelham.'

Kelham said: 'Worry me as much as you want to. Do you hear me?' His voice was taut, and his hands clenched. 'Catch the man who killed my son, that is all you need to worry about. Spare no one's feelings, least of all mine.'

He broke off, abruptly, and turned away. His gaze rested on a coloured photograph on the wall, the portrait of a young man very like him.

'I'll come in with you,' added Kelham, abruptly.

'Don't you think you'd better stay here?' asked Blair.

He broke off as Kelham shook his head and led the way to the hall again. A sergeant, Mellor, was waiting in the hall with the other detective-officer, and Willis came in from the sitting room; Kelham ignored the men and went to a closed door. The key was in the lock, and he turned it. He seemed to brace himself as he stepped inside, then stood aside for Roger.

Roger had rarely seen anything so uncanny. The large, flat-topped desk was placed in a position similar to that of the bureau in the other room, and Anthony Kelham was sitting at it, in a natural pose. His face was hidden, and from the angle he looked exactly like his father. One hand was flat on the desk, and his body was propped up by his other hand which gripped the edge.

He wore a light grey suit, and there was a small hole on the left front, the edges stained a brownish-red. His long dark hair fell over his forehead. When Roger touched his wrist it felt cold and stiff.

He turned. 'Was this exactly as you found him?'

'Exactly,' said Kelham. 'I noticed nothing unusual, and called out to him as I opened the door. Only when he failed to move or respond did I grow alarmed. I needed only a glance to see that he was dead. I felt his pulse; his wrist was already getting cold.'

'I see,' said Roger. 'Have you any idea who killed him, Mr Kelham?'

'I have not!'

'Do you know whether he had enemies?'

'To my knowledge he had none.'

'Who else knew that he was likely to be here this evening?'

'As far as I know, no one,' said Kelham. 'It wasn't until this morning that I heard he was coming here – he planned to spend Easter with his mother at our Newbury house, and I was going to join them for the weekend. He said that he had to come to London for the day and would spend the night here. I don't recall mentioning the fact that he was due to anyone except Blair.'

'I told no one,' Blair said, a trifle too quickly Roger thought.

'Do you know what brought your son here?' asked Roger.

'You had better read this,' Kelham said.

He handed Roger the note, crumpled at one corner, which he had held in his hand all the time. It was short and uninformative, written on Brasenose College paper in a poor hand, and it read:

Dear Andy,

Here's a pleasant surprise for you! I have to do one or two things in London tomorrow, and I doubt whether I shall be finished in time to get to Newbury tomorrow night, so expect me at five o'clock or thereabouts. All news when I see you, not that there's much!

Tony

'Thank you,' said Roger. 'I don't think there is any need for you to stay unless you have to, Mr Kelham. I can go into details later with Mr Blair, and the police surgeon will be here in a few minutes.'

'Is there any reason why I should not stay?'

'Not as far as I'm concerned,' said Roger.

'Then I will.'

During the next twenty minutes a dozen photographs were taken of the body from different angles, while Roger and Sergeant Mellor looked about the room. Roger did not examine the body until the doctor arrived. Dr Howard Winter was a youthful, clean-limbed man with an eager manner. Efficiency and a coldly inquisitive approach to cadavers were his chief characteristics.

He and Roger approached the body together. Before the brief inspection was over, Kelham changed his mind and went out of the room. Blair hovered near the door.

'There's not much doubt about what happened to him,' said Winter. 'Good shooting with a heavy-calibre revolver, eh? I think you'll find that death was instantaneous. I needn't stay any longer, need I?'

'No, thanks,' said Roger. 'Mellor, ring for the ambulance, will you, and warn the morgue at Cannon Row.' As the sergeant went out, Roger stepped to the door, and nearly trod on Blair's toe. 'Sorry,' he said perfunctorily.

He closed the door of the library, and got a smear of fingerprint powder on his hand, but photographs of the handle and of most of the furniture which had revealed prints had already been taken. Blair stood behind him in the passage. Roger opened the door slowly. It made no sound, and just cleared the thick carpet. When it was half-way open, there was a clear view of the desk and the dead man; a bullet fired from the waist would be on a level with the wound. He looked at the window, which was placed rather high. Two of the top panes were open, but he could see no way in which a bullet from there could hit a man at the desk.

Blair said, abruptly: 'It must have come from the door.'

'We take nothing for granted,' said Roger. 'Does Mr Kelham have to stay here?'

'Of course! He uses this as his office!'

'He won't be able to use this room in peace for a few days,' said Roger. 'It would be much more convenient if he were to move to a hotel, or to another flat – convenient for him, I mean. We can manage. Ask him, will you?'

While Blair was gone, Mellor came in and reported that there were no signs that the front door had been forced, and there were no scratches round the keyhole. Roger checked up on that, and spent five minutes looking at the other doors. A sergeant, Ling, came in to say that no one appeared to have seen Anthony Kelham arrive, nor heard the shot. By then the ambulance was at the gate. The manager of the block of flats was most anxious that the body should be taken out the back way, and Roger was amenable. He went into the sitting-room to see Kelham as the body was being removed.

Kelham was saying: 'If the police think it better then we can move. Don't be obstructive, Blair!'

'I was only thinking of your convenience,' Blair said stiffly. 'All your papers are here.'

'The police won't object to us moving some filing cabinets,' said Kelham, testily. 'Will you, Inspector?'

'Not after we've looked through them,' said Roger, 'to make sure they haven't been disturbed.'

'Why is that necessary?' demanded Blair.

Kelham swung on his secretary.

'I have had more than enough of your interference! Murder has been committed here, can't you get that into your head? The police will have to search thoroughly, will have to go through anything and everything. We shall afford them every possible assistance.' He looked at Roger, and his voice grew calmer. 'You must forgive me, Inspector, my nerves have been badly shaken. You won't mind if my secretary is here while you search?'

'Not at all,' said Roger.

'Thank you. I am making arrangements to go into a hotel for a few days.'

If Kelham had any reason to be afraid of the police, his acting was superb. It was probable that any incriminating papers had been removed before the police had arrived, of course. It was even possible that Kelham and Blair were putting up an act to deceive him. He would have considered that more likely but for Kelham's behaviour when he had first arrived. The man was more composed now, but his eyes had a glassy look, and his hands were clenched.

'There is one thing, Inspector. I would like to leave London forthwith, to see my wife. I can return tomorrow. She is not well, and cannot travel.'

'That will be all right,' said Roger.

'Thank you. Now, Blair. You fully understand that I wish for the utmost cooperation with the police in every way.'

'Yes,' said Blair, and added with an effort: 'What about your packing?'

'I will do it.'

'Oh, both of you can do it,' said Roger. 'I won't need to start on the cabinets yet.' He left them as they went into the bedroom, and spoke quietly to Sergeant Mellor. 'Have you got plenty of money in your pocket?'

'I've a pound or two,' said Mellor. 'Why?'

'Kelham's going out, and I want you to follow him.' Roger took out his own wallet, and extracted three pound notes, all he had with him. 'Borrow as much as you can from the others. As soon as you know his address for the night, telephone the Yard.'

'Right-ho, sir,' said Mellor. 'I won't lose him!'

'You'd better not,' said Roger. 'He's supposed to be heading for his country home – *Poplars*, Stratton, near Newbury. Have you got that?'

'*Poplars*, Stratton, near Newbury,' repeated Mellor.

'That's it. Scram!' Roger turned away and Mellor hurried downstairs.

Kelham had been gone ten minutes, and Roger began to look through the papers in the cabinet, when there was a ring at the front-door bell. A plainclothes man went to answer it, while Blair looked and muttered:

'I wonder who that is?'

Roger made no comment; the time for finding out why Blair was so jumpy would come later. He was revelling in this opportunity to study papers which had seemed quite inaccessible only a few hours before. Most of the papers appeared to be contracts, invoices and general correspondence, all connected with building or some branch of it. Blair glanced over his shoulder from time to time, and Roger could not put his mind to the job in hand while a man's voice alternated with a girl's in the hall.

Suddenly Blair swung round and hurried to the door.

Roger stood up and followed him.

Looking past Blair he could see a girl in a gaily-coloured mackintosh from which water was dripping. She wore a hood of the same material, and a fringe of damp fair hair showed at the sides of the hood. Roger saw her wide-open eyes, blue and bright as she looked in bewilderment towards Blair.

'Charles!' she exclaimed. 'What is the matter? What are these men doing here?'

She turned her gaze towards Roger, and demanded:

'Who are *you*?'

'I—' began Roger.

'He's dead!' cried Blair. 'Tony's dead. He's been murdered!'

CHAPTER THREE

Griselda

ALARM, dismay and perhaps a tinge of surprise showed on her pretty face, but she was not greatly astonished: that was the first thing he realized.

'Are you a policeman?' she asked, in a low voice.

'Yes,' Roger gave her his card, but she hardly glanced at it.

'Is Tony – is Mr Anthony Kelham dead?'

'I'm afraid it's true,' said Roger.

'Tony,' she said, and added: 'Poor, poor Tony!' She looked away from him, at Blair, who stood by a chair glaring at Roger, and seemed to have gone completely to pieces. 'Does – does Andy know?'

'Mr Kelham knows,' said Roger.

'I'm glad of that,' said the girl, and then added: 'I suppose you want to know who I am. My name is Fayne,

Griselda Fayne, and – and Tony and I were old friends.' She looked at Charles Blair, and Roger thought that she was rather contemptuous. 'I knew—'

'Why did you have to come?' cried Blair. 'Why on earth did you think Tony might be here, you knew he was going to Newbury. He—'

'But he told me that he'd be here,' said Griselda.

'He couldn't have done!' exclaimed Blair, wildly, 'he couldn't have done. Griselda, for heaven's sake, you—' He broke off.

'Don't be ridiculous,' she said, 'I didn't kill Tony.' She looked at Roger. 'That must sound a curious thing to say, Inspector—' a quick glance at the card followed, and she added: 'West. It isn't really. Tony and I have been on extremely bad terms, but we made it up on the telephone last night.'

'I see,' said Roger. 'Do you come here often, Miss Fayne?'

'Well, quite often,' said Griselda.

'Have you a key?'

'Oh, no, I'm not a member of the family.' She shot a glance at Blair, as if that remark was intended for a dig at him. 'It – it all seems so unreal,' she went on, 'I don't think I really believe it.' There was an uneasy pause. 'Well – can I see Andy?' she asked at last.

'He's gone to Newbury,' said Blair.

'Oh, of course, he would. Poor Mrs Kelham.'

Roger was curious about her use of Kelham's Christian name and the more formal 'Mrs Kelham'.

'I shall want to ask you one or two questions later, Miss Fayne,' he said, formally.

'Is that necessary?' she asked. 'I haven't seen Tony for weeks, and – but I suppose you know your business. I am at the Royal White Hostel, Buckingham Palace Gate. Charles, can I do anything for you?'

'No,' said Blair.

'You needn't be so ungracious about it,' said Griselda, turning on her heel. 'Please let me know as soon as Andy comes back, I must see him. Good night, Inspector.'

'We'd better get on with the job,' Roger said when she had gone.

Blair's agitation increased, but Roger pretended not to notice it, or his frequent glances towards the library door. After twenty minutes of unrewarded toil, Roger turned towards the door.

'I won't be a minute,' he said, and strode out without looking round, conscious of Blair's gaze. He went out, leaving the door ajar, and beckoned the detective officer, a heavily built man, who was still looking for fingerprints. He put his other hand to his lips, and the man tiptoed across the outer room as Roger flung the door wide open and re-entered swiftly.

Blair had some papers in his hand.

Quick as a flash, he thrust his hand into his pocket and rushed towards Roger, swinging his free arm wildly. Roger gripped his forearm and pulled his hand out of his pocket.

Several letters fell to the floor.

'You're a foolish fellow, Blair,' said Roger. 'Pick up those letters,' he added to the other man. 'I'll look after Mr Blair.'

He retained his grip, but Blair made no effort to break away, and stood staring at the letters as if hypnotized. Roger ignored the letters and pulled him towards the cabinet, saying tartly:

'I can't spend all night on this job!'

Blair gasped: 'Aren't you going to—' his voice trailed off, while Roger released him and took out another file of papers. It was marked: *Estimate – Bristol.* There was nothing likely to interest him in it, and he was fairly certain that the only papers which did hold interest for him were the letters on the desk. He did learn, however, that Kelham had an interest in several of the largest firms of building contractors, in brickyards and in subsidiary companies. There was hardly a part of the country affected by the slum-clearance programme in which he was not concerned. It was a mammoth enterprise.

He did no more than scan the documents; there was no

justification for doing more. It was after nine o'clock before he had finished, however, and he was feeling hungry.

It was Blair who broke the long silence.

'Look here, how long do you intend to stay here?' he demanded, with exasperation. 'It's late for dinner, and I'm hungry!'

Roger looked at him calmly.

'I'm afraid there isn't time to break off yet, Mr Blair, as there are one or two questions I wish to ask you. I think it would be better for you to come along with me to Scotland Yard.'

Blair cried: 'That won't be necessary, will it? I'll tell you whatever I can, I want to help, I—' he broke off, and then added: 'Damn you, give me a cigarette!'

Roger shrugged his shoulders, took out his case and, as Blair took a cigarette with trembling fingers, said quietly:

'You told Miss Fayne that Anthony Kelham would be here tonight. Whom else did you tell?'

'How – how did you know?'

'Your efforts to make her keep quiet about it were obvious,' said Roger, gratified at a successful shot in the dark. 'Whom else have you told?'

'No one!'

'Then *she* must have told someone,' Roger said.

'Don't be a fool!'

'Well, she either told someone else who came here and killed Tony Kelham, or else she killed him herself,' said Roger.

'That's utter nonsense!' snapped Blair.

'On her own admission, she had quarrelled with him.'

'I tell you they'd made the quarrel up!'

'I've only her word and yours for that,' said Roger. 'There's every reason to disbelieve her.' He was bluffing again, and again it worked.

Blair drew in a searing breath.

'I tell you you're wrong! She and Tony were engaged, until a few months ago, then they had a quarrel and broke it off. There's nothing unusual in that, is there?' Blair was speaking quickly, the words seemed forced from him. 'Griselda lost her temper, she—'

He broke off, and then cried:

'There's no need to start a scandal among Griselda's friends is there? She – she once nearly shot him. They'd quarrelled, and Tony said something pretty beastly. Gris – Griselda nearly always carries a gun, and – well, *any*one might have lost their temper. You can't blame her!' He drew in his breath, and then went on in a low-pitched, almost despairing voice.

It had happened at a small private party at the flat. Griselda and Tony Kelham had been on bad terms for some weeks, but Kelham was anxious to bring them together again, and had invited her without telling his son. Tony and Griselda had met in the library, each taken by surprise. The door had been open and several people had seen them. They had exchanged a few inaudible words, and then Tony Kelham had raised his voice and said, for everyone to hear, that she was the daughter of a criminal lunatic and ought to be shut up herself.

Blair said: 'I – I saw and heard it all, West, so did a dozen others. She – she went ashen, and stood looking at him for a moment, and then she – she snatched the gun out of her bag and fired at him. I was nearest. I saw what she was doing and rushed in, and the bullet went wide. We hushed it up, of course. Tony would never have been such a beast had he not been drunk.'

'I see,' said Roger slowly. 'Was the accusation about her father justified?'

'Yes. Her father died at Broadmoor. You'll be able to find out all about him in your records. But I tell you Griselda and Tony made it up. He tried to even that evening, he sobered up pretty quickly. She wouldn't listen, and went off, but he kept writing to her and telephoning her, and yesterday she agreed to let bygones be bygones. That's the gospel truth, West. Mr Kelham was always anxious to – to see them on good terms, he wanted them to marry. Naturally, I helped him.' The last words were barely audible.

Roger said, quietly: 'You found that difficult, Blair, didn't you?'

'It was damnable!' cried Blair. 'I worship the very ground she treads on, and I had to scheme ways of getting them together, had to – God forgive me if I've harmed her!' he added, and turning away sank into a chair and covered his face in his hands.

CHAPTER FOUR

The Girl Who Carried a Gun

WHILE BLAIR sat with bowed head, Roger went to the desk and, for the first time, read the three letters which Blair had tried to conceal. They were all typewritten, and bore neither address nor signature. He thought that the typewriter was the same as that used for the anonymous letters to Sir Guy; in any case it would be easy to make sure of that.

They were threatening letters, and the first, dated a month before, was typical of all three. It read:

If the police don't get you first, I'll put paid to your account, Kelham. You're living under the shadow of death. Any moment might be your last. The only reason I haven't killed you already is that I hope you'll be hanged, you devil.

When he had finished reading them, he glanced up to see Blair looking at him. The man's haggard face reflected the torment of his mind, and his eyes seemed to burn.

'Do you know who sent them?' Roger asked, suddenly.

'No.'

'Did Mr Kelham know they were in here?'

Blair muttered: 'He – he's never seen them.'

'*What?*' gasped Roger.

'I always open all his post,' said Blair, 'and he's got too much on his mind to worry about listening to the babbling of a lunatic! I – I always thought I might be able to find out who sent these, so I kept them here.' Blair eased his collar. 'I'm the only person who knew they arrived.'

'I see,' said Roger. 'Why were you so anxious to prevent me from seeing them?'

'I – I didn't want you to know that anyone had called him a murderer.'

'Is he a murderer? Roger asked, equably.

A tap at the door heralded a policeman with sandwiches and coffee. Blair first declared that he could not eat, but he set to with a will after eating one dainty sandwich, and drank coffee greedily. His gaze did not leave Roger, but it was not until his appetite was satisfied that he said:

'There isn't much more that I can tell you, West. If there's any truth in these accusations, it happened before I knew Andrew Kelham.

'Probably,' said Roger, 'but you're not familiar with all his current activities, are you?'

'I think so. I'm his confidential secretary. He doesn't go anywhere without telling me where he's going, as far as I know, and usually I go with him. There – there's one other thing that I suppose you'll have to know.' He paused. 'My father owned a small steel works, years ago. He wasn't well, and the business was failing. I – I was at Oxford. I knew nothing about his financial troubles until he died. Then I discovered that he was in debt to Andrew Kelham, who had foreclosed on the business. Within a few weeks the orders started coming in again and the works were prosperous. I came here feeling pretty vengeful. I would gladly have throttled Kelham, but to my surprise I found him very decent. I learned that he had offered my father a directorship on the new board. Well, the upshot of it was that I accepted the offer of a secretarial post from Kelham, and he's never failed me. That's the whole truth, West. I once hated the man bitterly, but I've come to love him.'

'Have you tried to find out who threatened him?'

'So far I've only toyed with the idea,' said Blair.

'Did Anthony Kelham ever receive similar letters?'

'I've never heard of any,' Blair said.

'Have you any theory at all as to why Anthony was murdered?'

'I – no, none at all,' said Blair.

'That isn't quite true, is it?' asked Roger. 'You have a shrewd idea that he was killed in mistake for his father. Isn't that so?'

'I can't imagine any other reason. You're pretty quick, aren't you?' said Blair bitterly.

'From some angles they're much alike,' said Roger. 'Do you think Mr Kelham believes that possible?'

'I don't know. He didn't say anything about it to me.'

'Right!' said Roger. 'That'll do for this evening – except that I'd like you to write a log of your activities today. And when it's done I'll have to ask you to leave this room. It will be locked up until we want it again.'

When he was alone in his office he wrote a brief report and then a list of inquiries to be made early next day.

One fact stood out clearly; the murderer had gained admittance to the flat by use of a key. He should have found out whether there was a master-key at the flats, held by the management, and he should have asked Blair who had keys to the flat. Presumably all the Kelhams and Blair had one apiece, and possibly the daily servant.

'Confound it!' exclaimed Roger, 'I've missed that point!'

He rang up Blair immediately and asked him for the woman's name and address; Blair gave it to him without hesitation, and told him that she had a back-door key. Roger looked at his watch; it was not much past ten o'clock, and there was still time to interview the woman. Her name was Ricketts and she lived in Lambeth, not five minutes' drive away from the Yard, on the fourth floor of an ancient tenement.

Roger sought a knocker unsuccessfully, and then banged with his fist.

'These places do stink, don't they?' whispered his driver, Gardener.

'Some of them,' said Roger, and banged again.

There was no answer, but a door opened on the top floor and a bedraggled-looking woman came down, followed by a younger woman dressed smartly; even in the gloom her bright lipstick was visible.

'Who d'jer want?' demanded the first woman, gruffly.

'Are you inquiring for Mrs Ricketts?' asked the second, politely.

'Yes,' said Roger. 'Isn't she in?'

'She *came* in—' began the younger woman.

'Shut yer trap, Lucy, and don't talk out of yer turn!' snapped the other. 'Wot jer want 'er for?'

'Just to ask her a few questions,' said Roger, pleasantly, and took out a card. 'I am from—'

'I know a busy when I sees one,' growled the older woman, clearly hostile. 'Worriting decent folks, that's wot yer up to.'

Gardener bridled, and Roger hastened to pour oil on the troubled waters. In a few minutes Lucy held the stage, and she had not finished speaking when Roger felt the first tremor of alarm. Mrs. Ricketts had returned from her work just after half past five, as she always did. According to custom, she and her daughter should have gone to supper with their upstairs neighbours; the two families had meals together on alternate evenings. Mrs Ricketts's daughter had gone to the pictures unexpectedly, however, and Mrs Ricketts had not put in an appearance. Lucy and her mother had banged on the door several times and received no answer; it was obvious that they were both puzzled and worried, for it was not their neighbour's habit to spend the evenings away from home.

Roger made no comment but simply put his shoulder to the door and pressed with all his weight. The lock groaned.

'Here, let me, sir!' cried Gardener.

He was a heavier man than Roger, and the lock gave way. While Gardener tried to keep the neighbours out,

Roger went into the tiny flat. Standing on the threshold of a dingy bedroom, Roger looked down at the body of Mrs Ricketts, by the side of the bed. She had been strangled.

Later that night Roger drove towards Chelsea slowly, his thoughts confused. The motive for the murder of Mrs Ricketts was obvious. The man who had shot Anthony Kelham had gone straight to Lambeth to stop her telling who had borrowed her keys. Yet he felt uneasily that this was one of those cases in which nothing was quite what it seemed.

The curtains at the house in Bell Street were drawn ,but there were several chinks of light. As he put the car into the garage at the back of the house, he reflected that Janet must have decided to wait up for him.

Janet opened the door and greeted him.

'You needn't have stayed up, Jan, I—'

'Is that Inspector West?' demanded another voice, and a second figure appeared and pushed past Janet; it was Griselda Fayne.

CHAPTER FIVE

A Story From Griselda

'HOWEVER urgent it is,' said Roger, firmly, 'I'm going to have a wash to freshen myself up. It's waited for so long that another ten minutes won't spoil it. I'll wash in the kitchen,' he added, for Janet's benefit.

Griselda Fayne's blue eyes were angry, but she raised no objection. On the way to the kitchen, Roger squeezed Janet's waist and kissed the lobe of her ear.

'I'm sorry about this, darling.'

'You couldn't help it.'

'How's Scoopy?'

'Fast asleep, bless him!' After putting on a kettle, she went on quickly: 'She arrived just after midnight. I told Bill Sloan that he'd better go when eleven o'clock came and you weren't back. Mark Lessing stayed to keep an eye on things. I went up to bed, and the knocking at the door woke me.'

'Did she say why she came?'

'Only that she wanted to see you.'

'I could help her at Scotland Yard as easily as I could here,' said Roger. 'I'm not fond of people who use Bell Street as an unofficial confessional.' He saw Janet's frown and laughed as he finished drying himself. 'Sorry, sweet, I'll treat her nicely! Sing out for Mark, will you?'

'*Mark!*' called Janet, obviously torn between making Mark Lessing hear and avoiding disturbing the baby. Mark heard, however, and came at once.

'Roger's got a down on her,' said Janet.

'That's too bad,' said Mark, 'but it's probably only because he's tired.' He grinned amiably at his friend.

He was a tall, spare-built man, with a chin too pointed and a nose too curved for good looks, yet he was impressive. His chief claim to fame were several small books on what he liked to call criminal lore, containing analyses of several spectacular cases; without them, he often said, the remarkable history of Chief Inspector West would never have been written. He declared modestly that he always liked to lend a hand, and most of the people at Scotland Yard respected him and valued his opinion.

'So it's only because I'm tired, is it?' asked Roger. 'We'll see. Do you know what's happened?'

'No,' said Mark and Janet, in unison.

'Her fiancé, or her ex-fiancé, was murdered tonight,' said Roger, 'and his name was Anthony Kelham.' He grinned at Mark's startled expression. 'I'm also told that she carries a gun. Get hold of her handbag on some pretext, Mark, and check up, will you? I can't, because I'm an officer of the law!'

'Leave it to me,' said Mark, confidently.

They let him go back alone, but both of them crept along the passage. He left the lounge door open, and they could just see Griselda standing by the piano and looking through an album of popular classics. Her blue leather handbag was on the piano.

He went straight in, put his hands on her shoulders and moved her to one side, opened the piano and played one or two notes, softly. Griselda was taken aback. Then Mark, turning over a page, knocked the album off, and she immediately bent down to get it.

Before she straightened up the bag was open, and in Mark's hand was a small automatic.

'Well, well!' he said, stupidly. 'What's this?'

Roger stepped into the room, with Janet pressing close behind him.

Griselda saw the open handbag and the gun, and her eyes blazed – and yet she stood quite still.

'I'll take charge of the gun until you produce your licence,' said Roger. 'Thanks, Mark. Miss Fayne, if you will be so unorthodox as to come and visit a policeman in his home, you must expect your motives to be suspect. I understand that you always carry this gun.'

She drew in her breath: 'Of all the beasts, Charles Blair is—' She stopped, took her bag from Mark's hand and closed it quickly. 'You probably won't believe me, but I came here to tell you about my quarrel with Tony and all that ensued.'

'Is that all you came to see me about?'

'No,' she said. She shot a glance at Mark, as if she felt that she could hope for moral support from him.

Janet said: 'I'll fetch the tea, Roger. I won't be a moment.'

She came back almost at once with the tea-tray and biscuits. Absently, Griselda accepted a cup, refused biscuits, and, between sips, she looked at Roger and said:

'You know that I' – a sip – 'nearly killed Tony Kelham a few weeks ago.' She sipped again. 'Do you know why?'

'I want you to tell me,' said Roger, evasively.

'That means that you do know. All right, Mr West, I will tell you my own version. Tony Kelham goaded me into a fury in which I would gladly have killed him, and I tried to kill him. He told the truth about my father, and that hurt. The truth,' she added, and caught her breath, then drank more deeply. 'He died in a lunatic asylum, to which he had been sent after he tried to commit suicide. He was driven to that, and probably to insanity, by – *Andrew Kelham!* He had a prosperous business. Kelham became a partner, and tried to buy my father out. In the end, father interfered with the accounts, and rendered himself liable to prosecution. So he tried – well, I needn't say that again. I suppose you're wondering why I allowed myself to become engaged to Anthony Kelham. I will tell you. I thought that through his son I might be able to avenge myself on Andrew Kelham.' She caught her breath. 'There have been times when I would gladly have killed them both!'

Roger said: 'You're certainly being frank.'

'I haven't finished. I was at the flat early this evening,' she said, in a toneless voice. 'I suppose I was the last person to see him alive.'

This was frankness with a vengeance, thought Roger, and he felt a sneaking shame because he had doubted the girl's sincerity.

'Why did you go to the flat, Miss Fayne,' he asked, gently.

'I just wanted to see Tony. We had made up our differences – I think he had done so genuinely, and I pretended to have done so. I did not know that he was coming to London until Charles Blair told me this morning. I got there just after five o'clock, and he admitted me himself. I left soon afterwards. I went home—'

'Do you mean to the hostel?'

'Yes. I'd arranged to meet him again at half past seven, and arrived a little early. Immediately I knew what happened I realized how it might look if you knew I'd been there before, and so I said nothing. After I'd thought about it I decided that I had been a fool, and I telephoned Scotland Yard. They said you had gone home, so I came here.' She looked defiant. 'That is the whole truth.'

'Apart from everything else, you've already helped,' said Roger, 'because we now have a fairly good idea of what time he actually reached the flat. Do you know if he'd been there long when you first came?'

'I think he'd only just arrived – he still had on his hat and coat. I know that I was there at five minutes past five, because I tried to get there exactly on the hour but was held up.'

'Why were you so anxious not to miss him?' asked Roger. 'On your own statement, you were not really fond of him.'

She stared at him, biting her underlip, not answering.

'Well, I can't make you talk,' said Roger. He took out the gun and examined it thoughtfully.

'He wasn't shot with that gun!' cried Griselda.

'You can hardly expect me to take your word for that,' said Roger.

'You don't need my word, you can tell by the wound, it—'

She broke off and bit her lip again, as Roger said grimly.

'How do you know the size of the wound, Miss Fayne?'

CHAPTER SIX

Griselda's Confession

IN a low voice, she said wearily 'I went back, and saw him dead.'

'How long after your first visit?'

'About a quarter of an hour.'

'So that establishes the time of the shooting,' said Roger. 'It was between five minutes and twenty minutes past five. That's useful, Miss Fayne.' His mild voice gave no warning of the question to follow. 'How did you get in the second time?'

'The door was open.'

'Are you quite sure?'

'Yes, I am! The door was unlatched and I went in and saw him sitting there. I thought at first that it was Andrew Kelham, and then I realized that it was Tony. I just turned and ran away. I knew that I would be suspected because of what had happened once before. But I couldn't keep away, so I came back and – and the sight of you scared me.'

'I'm afraid that story does not sound very plausible, Miss Fayne. In view of all the circumstances, I shall have to detain you,' Roger said, harshly.

Janet drew in her breath, and Mark stirred. The girl looked at Roger without speaking, but her cheeks were ashen again, and her hands began to tremble.

'Telephone the office for me, Mark, will you?' said Roger. 'And ask them to send someone over; any sergeant will do.'

Mark looked reluctant, and Griselda managed to say:

'You – you *can't* arrest me.'

A thunderous banging on the front door startled them all. Mark paused on the way to the telephone, and Janet glanced upwards, thinking of the baby. The knocking was repeated, and Roger moved towards the door, with Mark following him.

From upstairs there came the shrill wail of the child.

It was all hopelessly confused.

Janet screamed as Griselda Fayne rushed at her, swinging her bag. She sent her staggering to one side, and her cry reached Roger as he opened the front door and as Griselda reached the passage Mark half-turned, and received the handbag full in the face before Griselda ran along the lighted passage to the kitchen and slammed the door behind her. Janet had not recovered, the baby was now crying insistently, Mark and Janet banged into each other in the passage, and Roger could not give his attention to the man on the doorstep; he did notice that he was a very fat man.

'Is Miss Griselda Fayne here?' roared the fat man.

The baby's screams grew louder. Janet flew up the stairs. Mark hurried along to the kitchen, but found that the door was locked.

'Yes, she—'

He broke off, for in the faint moonlight he saw Griselda running quickly along the path which led from the back garden to the front. The fat man heard her footsteps and turned. Behind him was a second man, who immediately gave chase. In the road was a car or taxi, and the fat man swung round towards it.

Roger said: 'Whoever you are, I—'

'You have terrified her, sir!' roared the fat man, 'and I give you fair notice, you will rue the day when you filled her fair heart with terror!' He turned to face Roger and, without warning, gave him a terrific buffet across the face which made him lose his balance. The engine of the car started up. The fat man reached it and climbed in at the back; the car was moving away before Mark reached the gate or Roger had recovered. The footsteps of the man and the girl echoed faintly along the street.

'All *right*!' called Mark, joyously.

He made a flying leap at the car, which was reversing in the road, but the fat man struck out at him and Mark fell heavily into the road.

Roger needed no telling that further pursuit was useless. The car disappeared, and the last he saw of it was the dim glow of the rear lights. Griselda and the man chasing her had already turned the corner. There was just a chance of catching up with them, and he ran to the corner, but from there he could see no one.

Roger reached Scotland Yard the following morning, a little after half past nine, to find Eddie Day at his desk and two of his fellow inspectors reading the morning papers.

One of them looked up, and said with a grin that 'Handsome' had a good press. Roger had already seen the paper, in which the murder of Kelham's son had been given front-page headlines.

'Handsome!' said Eddie, 'you aren't half going to cop it one of these days, you mark my words. AC's been on the telephone *three* times for you already, and the last time he sounded as if he'd have your head, he did really.'

Roger laughed.

'Now look here, West,' said Chatworth, 'you must do better than this, you know. It's nearly ten o'clock, and I have been waiting to see you since nine. Now, let's forget it,' he added, brusquely. 'Have you checked Kelham and the man Blair?'

'I gave instructions for a check to start this morning, sir,' said Roger. 'I can give you a little more information about the time of the murder. We've established the fact that it was between five-five and five-twenty. I've had no reports in this morning yet.'

'How'd you know the time?'

'Miss Griselda Fayne told me,' said Roger, and launched into an explanation without saying when he had seen Griselda. Chatworth looked at him from beneath his shaggy brows, but did not interrupt.

'Hum, yes. What time did this scene with the girl occur,' he said, when Roger finished.

'Between one and two o'clock this morning,' said Roger, blandly.

'Then why the devil didn't you say so before?' demanded Chatworth. 'What else have you got up your sleeve, young fellow?'

'*I've* got nothing up my sleeve,' said Roger, virtuously, 'but I'm rather hoping that you have, sir.'

Chatworth said: 'Confound you, can't I call my thoughts my own! As a matter of fact,' he added, abruptly, 'certain Cabinet Ministers are a bit troubled by Kelham's increasing influence. It's very widespread. We had nothing else to bite on so I started you going. The death of his

34

son is a great help – callous way of looking at it, but there it is.'

When Roger left the office he wished rather ruefully that it were a more straightforward business.

'Were those letters typed on the same machine, Eddie?' he snapped as he entered his own room.

'Yes, they were. They were typed on a *Royal* portable, recent manufacture, or else one that hasn't been used much, because there were only two tiny flaws in the type,' Eddie went on, warming to his task. 'The "s" is a bit lower than the rest of the letters and the foot of the "i" is broken. Parky's going over them for prints, now.'

After telephoning and finding out that no one had yet come in with the reports, Roger sent a note through that anyone connected with the affair who had a *Royal* portable typewriter should be detained. Then he decided to visit Griselda's hostel.

Outside the hostel, which was an ordinary house in Buckingham Palace Gate with a notice-board outside, was a Yard man. He had nothing to report. Roger knocked at the door, a trim maid opened it, and in a few minutes he was talking to a matronly woman who wore pince-nez and her hair drawn tightly back from her forehead to a bun at the nape of her neck. She oozed efficiency, and her little office was neat and workmanlike.

'I should like to look at Miss Fayne's room,' he said, after introducing himself.

'It's *most* unusual,' said the matron.

'I could get a search warrant,' said Roger, 'but I don't want to make it as formal as that.'

'That's very thoughtful of you,' said the matron. 'Very well, Inspector, please come with me. I am *terrified* lest any of my staff should discover the presence of the police,' she went on as they walked along the passage and up the stairs. 'Already the man whom, I understand, you have stationed outside, has aroused their interest.'

It was a small room with one narrow window, a single bed, a dressing table, a small wardrobe and, by the window a typing desk with a standard machine on it. The keynote was tidiness. There were a few personal oddments, but for the most part the room had the look of a hotel bedroom and an office combined. There was one photograph on the dressing-table, of an elderly man.

Roger looked at it, and then at the desk. Standing by the desk was a portable typewriter in a case. As he picked it up, he saw the *Royal* trademark on a small label at the side.

CHAPTER SEVEN

More Evidence Against Griselda

GRISELDA FAYNE, it appeared, was a shorthand typist and secretary without a regular employer but with a select circle of clients. She was kept very busy, the matron told Roger, and frequently went out of London for two or three days. She was, if the matron was any judge, extremely efficient. So was Roger, who went through the drawers in the desk and found all the equipment that might have been expected, including an address book, a file of receipts and accounts, and a list of orders. There were also some manuscripts in longhand waiting to be typed. In spite of the matron's obvious uneasiness, he took the small typewriter, the address book, files and manuscripts away with him. As he walked to his car he almost banged into a man hurrying along with his head down.

'Sorry,' he said, and stood aside.

Before he realized the danger, the man swung round and punched him in the stomach. At the same time another man who had been at the opposite corner rushed across the road and hooked his legs from under him. As he fell, Roger let out a single piercing yell. The typewriter case hit the ground with a loud clatter, the lock burst and the typewriter itself showed in the open case. He saw that as one of the men kicked at his hand, and made him let go. The typewriter had saved him from the worst effects of the fall, and he squirmed forward, but one of the men thrust his head against the pavement and another began to pull at his coat sleeve. The papers he had taken from the hostel fell out.

A man snapped: 'That's them!'

Roger tried to twist round, to save the papers. He saw a hand shoot out and grab them, and was thumped on the side of the head. That put an end to his resistance. He heard heavy footsteps, and then the welcome sound of a police whistle. There were more footsteps behind him, and he knew that Gardener was on the way. A piercing blast on the whistle almost deafened him. Gardener raced past, without wasting time to inquire after him, and when he got up, unsteadily, he saw the man who had attacked him disappearing round the corner towards Sloane Square. The plainclothes man who had been on duty at the front of the hostel was lumbering across the road in pursuit.

Two or three people came up, and one started to brush Roger down. He had suffered no serious injury, although his nose felt tender, and when he touched it his finger was covered with blood. He dabbed at it with a handkerchief. Another good Samaritan picked up the typewriter, and said gloomily.

'Well, you haven't done that any good.'

They ran to the car only to find that the tyres had been slashed.

A cab was coming up, and Roger waved it down. He mutttered his thanks to his helpers, grabbed the typewriter and jumped into the cab, saying:

'I'm a police officer. Go towards Sloane Square.'

In a few seconds Roger, leaning out of the window and dabbing at his nose, saw one of his men still trundling along a side street, and Gardener, fifty yards ahead, racing in the wake of a small Morris car. As far as he could see, the driver of the car had stalled the engine and Gardener was gaining on it.

Roger snapped: 'Pick up that man and then follow the car.'

The taxi driver put on a burst of speed, then braked abruptly alongside Gardener. The little car had gathered speed and was twenty feet away. Roger saw Gardener make a flying leap for the taxi. He fell into it, Roger slamed the door, and the driver put on speed.

'*Gee-whiz!*' gasped Gardener. 'What a do!' as they sped west out of London.

'Looks like we're heading for Maidenhead,' said Gardener.

The effort to shake them off came in Reading, and Roger gave up all hope of keeping the little car in sight. He was going to tell the man to get to the Newbury Road when they swung round a corner, and, with people on the pavement crying out in alarm, caught sight of the Morris not thirty yards ahead of them. It managed to gain a few yards after a traffic block, however, and soon they turned on to the Newbury Road.

Suddenly a hand appeared at the side of the Morris and something hurtled through the air. It hit the ground a few feet in front of the taxi, and smashed. Pieces of glass hit the windscreen, and the driver wrenched his wheel, but went on.

'Your milk bottle,' said Roger, with a grimace.

The next moment there was the loud report as a tyre burst. The taxi lurched to one side, but the driver kept control. They wobbled to a standstill at the side of the road, and the little car turned a bend and disappeared from sight.

'Well, what a damned shame!' exclaimed Gardener. 'I do call that bad luck, I really do!'

Roger was too full for words. He opened the door and jumped down, but not before the taxi-driver had started to get the spare wheel out and the punctured tyre off. Gardener lent a hand, and within five minutes they had started off again. There was little prospect of catching up, however, and the cabby said:

'S'no use, I suppose. If I—'

'We'll go on as far as Newbury,' said Roger, 'they might be going to a house I know near there.'

They passed the drive gates of Kelham's house too swiftly for Roger to distinguish the name on them. As the taxi squealed to a standstill, a man came from the hedge and stared at them open-mouthed.

'Why *Inspector*!' gasped Sergeant Mellor. 'I never—' He stared at Roger's nose. 'I mean, here I am, sir, as instructed.'

'Good! Has a small Morris arrived here?' asked Roger.

'Haven't seen one,' said Mellor, 'but it might have gone the other side, sir, there are two drives. You can't see what happens on the other side, because the house is on the hill, as you see.'

'Yes. Is Kelham still here?'

'As far as I know,' said Mellor.

'Good! Mellor, show Gardener where to go to get the best view of both drives. Gardener, do you know Mr. Andrew Kelham by sight?'

'Yes, sir.'

'Signal to Mellor if you see him leave by the other drive,' said Roger. 'You might tell Gardener who else we're looking for, Mellor. All right, driver, up to the house, please.'

It was an attractive-looking house of reddish-yellow brick, with a red-tiled roof and gables. He had never met Mrs Kelham and had often wondered why she never came to London. Kelham had said for some time that she was in poor health, but it was surely a serious illness if it kept her indoors all the time.

He rang the bell, still feeling a little breathless.

A young maid opened the door.

'Is Mr Kelham in?' asked Roger.

'I think he's engaged, sir' said the maid. She stood aside for Roger to enter, and asked him his name. He was on the point of handing her a card when he heard a booming noise from upstairs. He looked up sharply. A door had opened and the voice grew louder.

'I give you my word, Andy, it will not do, it just will not do!'

'I don't think—' came Kelham's voice, much quieter; then apparently the door closed and Roger did not hear what followed. The maid was looking at him expectantly, and he drew his hand from his pocket and, choosing a name at random, said:

'Gardener, George Gardener. I have a message from Miss Fayne for him.'

'If you will please take a seat, sir, I will tell Mr Kelham,' said the maid.

As he watched her walking up the wide staircase, he was pondering on the fact that the booming voice belonged to the fat man whom he was so anxious to meet.

CHAPTER EIGHT

The Fat Man is Indignant

AFTER a short interval the maid returned.

'Mr Kelham will be engaged for the next twenty minutes or so, sir,' she said. 'Will it be convenient for you to wait?'

'Yes, thank you,' said Roger.

He had seen which upstairs room the girl had entered, and he stepped to the opposite side, so that if Kelham or the fat man looked out to see who he was, they would be disappointed. He could just see the bottom of the door, however, and he saw it open; he thought he heard a whisper before it closed. It opened again in a very few minutes, and this time he saw a man's feet. He thought it was the fat man, although he could only see the bottoms of his trousers and his highly-polished shoes. The fellow tiptoed, and was obviously intent on coming to the banisters to peer down.

Roger stepped forward swiftly and sat in an easy chair, with his back to the landing; he doubted whether either the fat man or Kelham would recognize him. Faint, furtive movements continued to come from the landing, and he thought he heard a whispered: 'Confound the fellow, he's sitting down!'

Then the door closed again.

Roger jumped up, looked about him to make sure that he was not observed from anywhere else, and dashed silently up the thickly carpeted stairs.

He stepped close to the door.

'I tell you I've never heard of the fellow. Gardener? Griselda knows no one named Gardener. I am sure of that.' It was the fat man.

'You're talking nonsense,' said Kelham, irritably. 'This man has probably heard from her.'

Roger thought: 'So she got away from the fat man!'

'I'm going to see who it is,' Kelham said, firmly.

The door opened, and Kelham stopped on the threshold, startled. He recognized Roger on the instant, and Roger thought that alarm mingled with his surprise. There was a short, tense silence. Then:

'Good morning!' said Roger, brightly.

'What does this mean?' snapped Kelham, angrily. 'I understood you to say that your name was Gardener, Inspector.'

There was an explosive sound from the fat man, whose shadow was visible on the wall by the door. It moved suddenly, and Roger, determined not be denied an interview, pushed past the startled Kelham. A door, obviously leading to the next room, was closing, and he heard the lock snap.

'West!' cried Kelham.

'Excuse me,' said Roger, and pushed past him again into the passage. He slammed the door, and then stood quite still, hearing Kelham move across the room, but look-

41

ing towards the next door along the passage. It was opening slowly. He pressed close against the wall as the door opened wider and the fat man peered out.

'*Alexander!*' came Kelham's voice in an urgent whisper.

The fat man started, but Roger stepped forward swiftly and, before the fat man could close the door, reached it and put his foot against it.

Beyond the fat man he could see Kelham at another open door. Kelham looked alarmed, while the fat man, a truly enormous fellow, back slowly away, staring at Roger fixedly.

'Haven't we played hide-and-seek enough?' demanded Roger.

'Who – who is this man?' demanded the fat man, in a piping voice. 'Andy, do you allow such gentry to roam at large about your premises? Am I mistaken, or is this fellow here without any right? Is he not, in fact, trespassing?' His voice grew deeper as he recovered his composure, and Roger admired his presence of mind.

'You know who I am,' said Roger. 'I haven't forgotten your strong-arm stuff last night, Mr Alexander.'

Kelham said:

'Inspector, I must request you to leave my house immediately. I shall complain to your superior about your unwarrantable intrusion.'

'Let us ask him, rather, why he told us so untruthfully that he had a message from poor Griselda,' said the fat man. He moved forward with his hands outstretched, his lips parted, his whole expression one of incredulous hope. 'My dear sir, I beg you to be frank!' There was a catch in his breath. 'I beg you to be *wholly* frank. Have you tidings of my niece? Can you tell me where to find Griselda Fayne?'

'I wish I could,' said Roger.

'So – she is lost, poor child, she is lost,' said Alexander, and he resumed his former pose. 'I was afraid of it. A reckless child as far back as I can remember, always headstrong, never amenable to avuncular discipline. Poor, poor child. My heart grieves for her.'

Kelham frowned, and looked at Roger as if to say that it was obviously impossible to expect any sense from Mr Alexander.

'Inspector,' he asked, 'exactly what brought you here?'

Roger said: 'Two men robbed me after I had visited Griselda's room and taken some papers away. I followed them here.'

'Here!' cried Alexander. 'The damned fools!'

'Why, did you tell them to go elsewhere?' asked Roger, sweetly.

Afterwards, he admitted that he should not have allowed himself to be taken by surprise. Jubilation was the main cause of his momentary carelessness; in wringing that involuntary sentence from Alexander he had completely vindicated himself. While he was rejoicing, Alexander pushed Kelham on one side and leapt at Roger. A single sweep of his mighty arm was enough to send Roger to one side, and then he ran to the door and pulled it open. He was halfway down the stairs before Roger reached the landing.

Kelham hurried in Roger's wake.

Roger saw no chance of catching up with the man unless he could somehow delay him. He looked round swiftly, but the landing was almost bare of movable objects. Alexander, now near the foot of the stairs, was glancing over his shoulder. Roger turned, and slipped on one of the Persian rugs. As he recovered an idea entered his head. He picked the rug up, folded it double, and threw it towards the front door. It unfolded and floated slowly towards the end of its journey. For a moment it hid Alexander from sight, although as he ran down the stairs Roger saw the man try to strike it away from him.

It was Alexander's one mistake, for the rug coiled about his arm, and when he tried to shake it free, fell about his head and shoulders. He rushed forward blindly, but caught his foot against the door mat and banged heavily against the front door.

Roger slowed down.

It looked as if the blow had winded Alexander, but he was wary as he approached. The man made no further effort to get the rug away from his arm, but he pulled it from his face and stood by the door, breathing heavily. The absurd pompous expression was gone from his face. He looked malignant and angry.

'What the devil is the matter with you?' demanded Kelham, breaking a short silence. 'West will think you're crazy if you go on like this!'

'No,' said Roger. 'Not crazy.' He pulled Alexander away from the door, and the man made no further effort to attack him. He opened the door and put the police whistle to his lips. It echoed loudly through the hall, and startled the others. Before he left the open door, he saw two figures begin to move up the drive. The taxi-driver was staring at him in some alarm.

'It's all right,' Roger called to him, and turned again to Alexander. 'So you think they were fools to come here, do you?' he said. 'I'm talking of your two men in the car. You aren't very clever, Mr Alexander.'

He did not finish.

From Alexander's mouth there came a curious gurgling sound, and in front of Roger's eyes he began to change colour. His lips were tinged with blue, the florid red of his cheeks grew pasty, and his eyes began to roll. He held his hands rigidly by his side, clenching and unclenching them, until suddenly he moved one to his throat and began to clutch it. At the same time he swayed from side to side, and the gurgling shaped itself into words:

'Pocket – waistcoat pocket—'

Kelham moved swiftly to his side. Roger, wary and yet finding it hard to believe that this was feigned, steadied him. Kelham ran through his waistcoat pockets, and, with an exclamation, drew out a small glass phial. By then Alexander was leaning his full weight against Roger, who had difficulty in preventing him from falling. Kelham saw what was happening, and between them they half-carried and half-dragged the fat man to a settee. The springs groaned as his great weight fell on them.

His mouth was opening and closing like a fish's, and he kept gurgling. Kelham shook a tablet from the phial to the palm of his hand, and as he held it up, Alexander nodded violently.

'Get some water,' Kelham snapped.

Roger went to the service door, flung it open, and bellowed for a maid. One came running into the hall.

'Water, quickly,' said Roger.

The maid took one frightened glance at Alexander, and disappeared into a cloakroom. By the time she had returned with a glass of water, Mellor and Gardener had reached the porch. They stared at Alexander without speaking, and Roger said:

'Come in, and stand by.'

By then Alexander had swallowed the tablet and drunk the water. He sat gasping for breath, his face now quite blue. The whole party stood staring at him until Kelham said to the maid:

'All right, Mary.'

The girl hurried away, and Kelham looked at Roger with an apologetic smile.

'I should have warned you about this, West. He's liable to these attacks if he receives a shock.'

Roger said: 'It looks as if he's going to get a lot of attacks in the near future.'

Kelham frowned.

'I wish you hadn't said that. Will you come upstairs to my study for a few minutes?'

'Don't let Mr Alexander leave the hall,' Roger ordered, and then went with Kelham, who did not speak until they reached the study. Kelham drew his hand over his hair; he looked tired and troubled.

'I know that you are finding it most trying,' he said. 'I suppose I haven't helped, but you startled me when you gave a false name, and I was angry – justifiably, I think. However, that isn't important now. Alexander is. He is a wealthy eccentric and a close friend of mine, and I humour him in every way I can. I don't want to labour the word "eccentric" too much, but—' he broke off.

45

'Are you trying to tell me that he's insane?' asked Roger, bluntly.

'I wouldn't go so far as that,' said Kelham. 'He isn't quite normal, and he is given to these outbreaks of violence and to these sudden heart attacks. He's too fat, of course – he weighs over twenty stone.'

Roger said: 'I don't know whether he's certifiable or not, but I do know that his behaviour is highly suspicious. I'm afraid I shall have to take him away with me.'

'What exactly have you got against him?' asked Kelham.

'The fact that he assaulted me last night, and knew that Griselda Fayne had come to see me,' said Roger.

Kelham said: '*Did* she do that?'

'Yes.'

'She is an astonishing child,' said Kelham, and shrugged his shoulders. 'No one has ever been able to predict what Griselda would do next. However, that's by the way. You're quite wrong about Alexander assaulting you last night, I assure you. He was here when I arrived, a little after eleven o'clock, and he hasn't left the house since then.'

CHAPTER NINE

Return to London

ROGER did not believe him, but he did not say so.

Kelham looked relieved.

'I suppose all fat men do look rather alike, after dark,' he said. 'Why did you come here, Inspector? Not to see him, I assume?'

'No – the two men I've mentioned came near here,' Roger said, and dismissed the subject. 'I must get back to

London soon, but while I'm here, what can you tell me about Griselda Fayne?'

'She is the daughter of a man whom I knew in business,' said Kelham. 'Her father was in difficulties, tried to take his own life and was violent with his friends. He died in a criminal lunatic asylum. I've always tried to help her – she is a bewitching little creature, as you've doubtless noticed. She isn't in serious trouble, I hope?'

'I want to ask her a few questions,' said Roger.

'In connexion with my son's death?'

'Yes. She saw him last night.'

'Oh,' said Kelham. 'I begin to understand you. I expect you have discovered that unfortunate incident when she pretended to shoot at Anthony. I think you will make a mistake if you take that as a precedent, and I hope you will go very carefully.'

'I will,' said Roger.

'Good! Well, Inspector, we seem to have got as far as we can. You'll want to leave your men here, I suppose; but don't let the poor fellows hang about outside, they're quite welcome in the house.' He smiled, faintly. 'Neither Alexander nor I will try to run away, I assure you. Oh – will it affect your plans if I don't return to London until later in the day, or even tomorrow morning? My wife received a very great shock, of course, and I am very anxious about her.'

'Make it later today, if you can,' said Roger, brusquely. 'Now, I'd like to see Mr Alexander again.'

Downstairs in the hall, Alexander was sitting forward on the settee. The blue pallor had gone, and his face was pasty. The twitching had also gone, and he was talking in a subdued voice to Gardener and Mellor; Gardener seemed fascinated.

'It must indeed be a remarkable vocation,' Alexander was saying. 'Service to the community at large,' repeated Alexander, with bated breath. 'The hounding down of unscrupulous criminals, so as to make the life and property of the people safe.' He gave a slow, sad, smile. 'Ah me, life is rarely what you expect it to be! I will confess that in my

47

youth I dreamed great dreams. I wished to become a police-man. The dignified mien and the impressive uniform fas-cinated me. Little did I think that the ebb and flow of fortune would make the realization of my ambition imposs-ible!' He looked up as Roger and Kelham reached the hall, and his face brightened. 'Andy, my dear fellow, I wondered how long you would be! And Inspector – *West*, is that the name? To what great eminence *you* have risen!' he cried loudly. He stood up unsteadily, and took a step forward.

'Andy, tell me the truth. Was I—' Alexander paused, and then whispered the last word: '*Violent?*' When Kelham did not deny it, he drew in his breath, and turned to look at Roger with a pathetic stare. 'I am terribly sorry, Inspector, *terribly* sorry.'

'Oh, that's all right,' said Roger, brusquely.

'Come upstairs,' said Kelham to Alexander, and then he added: 'What about lunch, Inspector? Will you join us?'

'No, thanks,' said Roger, 'but if you can find some for my men, they'll be grateful.'

'I will see to it,' said Kelham. 'Goodbye for the pres-ent.'

Alexander was already halfway up the stairs, walking heavily and looking thoroughly dejected. Roger stood so that he could see the man's profile, but nothing in his ex-pression suggested that he was acting. He disappeared with Kelham, and the study door closed.

'Well, I'm—' began Gardener.

'Don't say it,' said Roger. 'I know. I don't think Alexan-der is the sick man he pretends to be, and I don't trust anyone in this house. I shall want a full and detailed report on everything that happens. Gardener, you come back with Kelham – and you, Mellor, stay until I recall you, and keep a look-out for Griselda Fayne or either of those fellows who attacked me at Victoria. Gardener saw them.'

Only Eddie Day was in the office, and he had no infor-mation and no dire warnings. He grimaced when he saw the typewriter case, but when Roger took the machine out, he found that although the enamel was chipped it was in working order. Roger could not work up any feeling of excitement when he typed a few sentences and, with Eddie Day breathing down his neck, compared the typewriting with that of the anonymous letters.

'That's it!' cried Eddie.

He spotted the broken 'i' and the 's' which was out of alignment, and his cry made Roger's heart jump.

He went along to Chatworth's office, and Chatworth gave him a one-sided grin.

'I hear you've been in the wars, West!' He stared at Roger's nose, over which a new skin had formed but which was red and puffy.

'I have, sir,' said Roger, 'and I don't feel very proud of it. I lost some papers which I took away from Griselda Fayne's room, and it seems as if they were of great importance.'

'Well, it's no use crying over spilt milk,' said Chatworth. 'You've been to Newbury, haven't you?'

'Yes,' said Roger, and explained at some length.

Chatworth listened intently.

'And that's as far as I've got,' said Roger at last. 'There's just one other thing, sir.'

'What's that?'

'This is a curious business, and it might be useful to have outside help. I'm thinking of—'

Chatworth grinned. 'Your friend Lessing!'

'Lessing and Pep Morgan, sir,' said Roger.

'Hum. Why call on a private agency to help in this?' asked Chatworth, frowning.

Roger said, slowly: 'I'm worried about Kelham, sir. He knows all – our people fairly well by now, and Blair knows them also. I'm not suggesting we employ Morgan at once, but I would like to be able to call on him in an emergency.'

'Oh, all right, all right,' said Chatworth.

Something like a deep depression settled on Roger in the next two hours. He telephoned Pep Morgan, a little agent with whom he had often worked. Another disappointment: Morgan was out.

* * *

He reached home a little before seven o'clock.

No depression was so deep, these days, as to withstand the cajolery of Master Martin West. He was lying on a chair near the fire, regarding his fingers with wide-eyed interest.

Suddenly, the baby caught sight of Roger.

'Hallo, there!' said Roger, beaming. He poked him gently in the tummy, 'Hallo, Scoopy!'

'Dar-*ling*!' came Janet's voice. 'Supposing I ask Mrs Norman if she'll sit in for the evening, and we go out to the pictures? She said only today she would gladly come in, and she's had three of her own, so I'm quite happy about leaving him with her. Shall we?'

'Bless you, yes,' said Roger.

It was a scramble to get ready, but the kindly neighbour proved willing and just after eight o'clock they were holding hands at the local cinema. Loud rhythmic music was playing in the interval, and it was faded abruptly as the curtains were drawn back; but instead of the title of the feature film, a notice was flashed on the screen.

'Roger!' cried Janet. 'Scoopy!'

For the message read: *'Will Inspector and Mrs West please return home at once?'*

CHAPTER TEN

Threats in the Night

THEY stumbled over the feet and knees of the other people in the row, Janet leading the way, Roger apologizing freely. Janet started to run towards the exit, and tripped up over a step.

They burst through the swing doors to the brightly-lit foyer, and a commissionaire opened the street doors.

'Roger – look – a taxi!' cried Janet.

'Taxi!' yelled Roger.

The cab pulled up, and Janet climbed in while Roger gave the address. As he did so, a man came out of the darkness by the side of the cinema, and asked:

'Is that you, Mr West?'

'Oh darling, don't wait,' implored Janet.

'You carry on,' said Roger, 'you won't have any peace of mind until you've seen him. Off you go, driver!' He turned to the man by his side, feeling certain that he was from the Yard and that the Yard had sent the SOS. 'Well, what's all this about?' He did not recognize the man, and peered into his face, which was in shadow. 'Who are you?'

'Never mind who I am,' the man said. He was by Roger's side, and something was poking into Roger's waist. 'Don't argue and don't waste time, West. Go that way!'

Roger went rigid. 'I—!'

'I'll blow you apart if you don't move on!' said the other, fiercely.

They reached a side-street.

'Down here,' said the man who was poking the thing against Roger's ribs. He had no choice but to obey.

Two other men were waiting, and they hustled him down the street.

A small wooden shed loomed up, and one of the men released him and went ahead, opening the door with a key. If he were to break away, he would have to take the chance now. He stiffened again, but they were extremely watchful, and the man with the gun – if it were a gun – pushed him forward. In a moment he was being hustled into the shed.

They closed the door before switching on a light; it was a poor one, from a shadeless lamp hanging from the wooden ceiling. The hut was empty. It had a concrete floor, and the walls were hung with dirty cobwebs. There was a musty, unpleasant smell that made him cough.

Now he could see his captors: a bald-headed man of medium height, with a round, good-humoured face; a tall, thin man and the smallest of the trio, a thick-set fellow with a rugged face.

Now there was no doubt that he had a gun; a Luger automatic was pointed at Roger's stomach.

'Now what's all this about?' demanded Roger, forcing himself to keep his voice calm. Surely if murder was their object they would have killed him by now.

The man with the gun said:

'Listen, West. You're after a girl called Griselda Fayne. She's a nice girl. She's a friend of mine. If you arrest her, you'll make trouble for yourself. Do you understand?'

'Yes,' said Roger.

'What have you got against her?'

'She was at the Kelham flat when young Kelham was murdered,' said Roger. 'At least, just before and just after it.'

'What else?'

'Nothing.'

'Then why did you take the papers from her room?'

'You made a mistake there, Baldy.'

The bald-headed man started. '*What?*'

'Until you snatched those papers I didn't know they were important,' said Roger. 'I do know now.'

The bald-headed man said, uneasily: 'I told you—'

'Shut up!' said the man with the gun. 'Listen to me, West. You're a man as well as a policeman, a family man. You've got a wife and you've got a kid.' His sneer widened, and Roger started. 'Well, if you want to make sure your wife and kid don't get hurt, ease off Griselda and forget what we look like. Okay, Sam!'

The thin man seemed to have been waiting for that word. Something struck the side of Roger's head and he slumped into unconsciousness.

Within two minutes the shed was locked on him, and he was alone.

At first, Janet's relief at seeing Mrs Norman sitting in an easy chair with a magazine, and at finding the baby asleep in his cot, had been her only emotion, but by midnight she was a prey to all sorts of fears, and she could no longer resist the temptation to call the Yard.

She asked for Roger, and was told that he had not been in since half past six.

'But he has been!' cried Janet. 'There was a message for him, and he went back.'

'I haven't heard about it, Mrs West,' said the operator, 'but I'll make inquiries. Hold on, please.'

Eventually Inspector Sloan, who had been at the house the previous evening, came on the line. Within a few seconds he was as worried as Janet, for he was quite sure that no message had been sent to the cinema. He promised to put inquiries in hand immediately, told Janet to cheer up, and replaced the receiver. Janet straightened up, and stared at the clock. Suddenly, she dialled another number, and she heard the ringing sound for a long time.

At last, a gruff, sleepy voice answered.

'Lessing here. Who'ssat?'

'Janet. Mark, can you come over right away? Something's happened to Roger, something mysterious, and I just can't stand being here on my own tonight. Can you come?'

'I won't be twenty minutes,' Mark assured her. 'Jan, there's nothing badly wrong, is there? Roger hasn't been hurt?'

'I don't know where he is,' wailed Janet. 'I—'

Then she broke off abruptly, for there was a thud in a room upstairs. She gasped: 'Mark, hurry, there's someone here!' and, without replacing the receiver, she flew out of the room and up the stairs to the nursery.

The cot was empty.

'Oh, please God, don't let him be harmed!' she breathed.

There were footsteps outside, running away. She went to the window, which was wide open, and with every ounce of breath she shouted:

'Help! Help! *Police!*'

She shouted again, and saw a light appear in a window opposite. It opened, and the silhouette of Mrs Norman's head and shoulders appeared.

'What is it, Mrs West?'

53

'Oh, please come!' cried Janet. 'Please come! They've taken Scoopy, they've taken Scoopy!'

She could not speak again, and turned from the window and raced down the stairs. Perhaps they had a car waiting outside. She reached the front door and opened it. There was nothing to be seen and the footsteps no longer sounded. Mrs Norman came hurrying with her husband, a middle-aged couple in dressing-gowns and slippers; the man's hair was standing on end.

Janet gasped: 'I heard a noise, and – he's gone, he's gone!'

'Come along, my dear,' said Norman. He gripped her arm and led her back to the house. 'Nothing serious will happen, you needn't worry,' he added, and in spite of the emptiness of the words they had a steadying effect. 'Sit down,' said Norman, and pushed her into an easy chair. 'Now, take a sip of this, my dear.' He unscrewed the top of a small flask of whisky he had brought and wiped it with deliberate care. 'Now, head back!' he put one hand beneath her chin, and added in an aside to his wife: 'Go upstairs and look in all the bedrooms, Nora.'

'I must go!' said Janet.

'Sit down!' said Norman, and forced a little whisky into her mouth. 'There's nothing you can do that Nora can't; now, sit down.'

As she swallowed the whisky, Janet felt giddiness and faintness overwhelm her, and all colour ebbed from her cheeks. Norman's portly figure seemed to be moving in rapidly widening circles. Above the droning in her ears she seemed to hear the frenzied cries of her child. She sat gripping the arms of the chair, in an agony of mind which seemed to affect every nerve and sinew.

Then from upstairs there came a cry:

'He's here! He's all right!'

'No!' cried Janet. 'No! I—' She jumped up and raced to the door and up the stairs.

Mrs Norman was standing by the open door of her bedroom – and when Janet reached the door, she saw the child sleeping in the middle of her own bed.

CHAPTER ELEVEN

More News of Griselda

'I CAN'T understand it,' said Janet to Mark Lessing, who had just arrived. She had the baby in her arms, and it was awake and looking steadily at her. 'Why on earth should they *pretend* to take him? The devils! I've never been so tortured, it—' She drew in her breath. 'Someone must look for Roger. It must be connected with him, it must be.' She looked down at the baby, and then said firmly: 'I can't help it, he'll have to sleep in my room tonight, and I won't leave him. Will you wheel the cot in, Mark?'

Twenty minutes later, she was much calmer. Two aspirins with a cup of tea had helped to steady her, and there was a tinge of colour in her cheeks. She was smoking a cigarette, a thing she rarely did, and looking anxiously at Mark. Mrs Norman had gone next door to get a warmer dressing-gown for her husband, who was on guard outside the bedroom door.

Mark had telephoned the Yard again, and explained exactly what had happened. He had been assured that a thorough search was being made for Roger, and that any news would be telephoned as soon as it came in.

'There's just nothing more we can do,' said Mark.

Footsteps sounded in the street, and stopped at the gate. The gate opened and then slammed.

'I expect the Yard has sent someone along, and he's pretty sore at being woken up,' said Mark. He reached the door, opened it, and then gasped: '*Roger!*'

Roger stood on the step, bruised, tired, his clothes torn and dirty.

'Roger!' cried Janet, and flew to him.

'All safe and more or less sound, you see,' he said with a grimace, 'but have I got a headache! Could there be a cup of tea?'

'Of course,' said Janet. 'We've just had some.'

Roger's eyebrows shot up. 'Here, what is this? What brought you, Mark? And why does Janet look so—' He broke off as he heard footsteps in the hall, and then saw Mrs Norman with a dressing-gown over her arm. 'Jumping jackanapes, what *is* going on here?'

'We've had a bit of a shindy,' said Mark, 'but it's all right now.'

Then Janet let loose a flood of words, to which Roger listened with a set face. When she had finished, he said slowly:

'So that's a warning of what we can expect. I'll have a hundred men in the house until this show's over,' he added savagely.

'Now don't get worked up, Mr West,' said Mrs Norman. 'My husband's on guard upstairs.'

'Eh?' exclaimed Roger, bewilderedly. 'On guard – oh, I see. You *are* a good couple! We needn't keep you up any longer, though, and I feel quite sure there is no need to expect further trouble tonight. There's one way in which you can help us, though, Mrs Norman. I'd like to put one or two men in your house tomorrow, to keep an eye on ours. They won't be in the way, I assure you. No one would know that they were there, of course, or what they were doing.'

'Why, that's simple,' said Mrs Norman, and called upstairs, 'Ted! Ted, it's all right, you can come off duty.'

A few minutes after the Normans left, two plainclothes men arrived from Scotland Yard, and looked startled when Roger admitted them. He remembered then to telephone the Yard with descriptions of the three men. When that was done, he wondered whether it would be wise to get in touch with the manager of the cinema that night, but decided to leave it until the morning. He stationed the Yard men in the sitting-room with strict instructions to call him if there were any kind of alarm, and then went to bed. Mark stayed again.

Roger was woken by the *rat-tat* of the postman. One of the

Yard men opened the door, signed for a registered packet, and called up to ask what he should do with it. Roger asked him to bring it up, and took it from him on the landing.

It was a small envelope, heavily sealed with red wax, and with a typewritten address, marked: *Personal to Inspector West*. He glanced into the bedroom. Janet was still asleep, although the baby was murmuring, quite happily, to himself. It was nearly seven o'clock, and getting light.

Mark appeared at his door.

Roger opened the packet, and found that it consisted of folded sheets of blank typewriting paper. He unfolded them one after the other, frowning and suspicious, and found some typewriting on the last sheet. He opened it out, and read:

> By now you know how easy it will be, West. This is being posted before we've talked to you or visited your house, but we know just what we're going to do, and we'll do it. We don't want to hurt your wife or child, but—

Roger smiled twistedly, and handed it to Mark.

'They're confident, aren't they?'

'They're fools,' said Mark, briefly. 'No one but a fool would think that they could frighten a Yard man, and even if they thought you'd back out, they ought to know that the rest of the Yard would soon be after them.'

'That's only half the story,' said Roger. 'Obviously they think that I know something which no one else does. They don't want me to pass it on.'

'Do you know anything?'

'If I do, it's unconsciously,' said Roger. 'One thing is established,' he added with a grin, 'they're badly worried. We always knew that this was a big business, but it's nice to know that we have them on the run. Will you bath first, or shall I?'

Soon afterwards Martin's cries grew loud, and Janet woke up and went down to get his bottle. Roger bathed and shaved, and then went down to the telephone. He sent the two men off for some breakfast, and told them to come back within an hour; they had slept in turns, and assured him that they were quite fresh. By the time Janet had prepared breakfast, he had spoken to the Yard again, but obtained no information. He also arranged with Pep Morgan's firm to send two agents to Mrs Norman's house, telephoned Mrs Norman to say what time they would arrive, and then, after much trouble, managed to find the private number of the manager of the cinema.

That worthy was still in bed, and surly on being woken up. His manner changed when Roger said crisply:

'This is Chief Inspector West of New Scotland Yard speaking. Can you hear me, Mr Lovelace?'

'Eh? Scotland Yard. Oh yes, yes.'

Five minutes afterwards Roger replaced the receiver. The story was simple. A man had telephoned the manager the previous evening, just after half past eight, said he was a police inspector, and asked for the message to be flashed on the screen. The manager had not given it a second thought, for a similar request had come before. The only additional fact that Roger discovered was that the call had come from a private telephone and, the manager thought, through an extension. The first man had asked him to hold, and he had heard what he thought was the extension line being rung. A crisp and decided voice had given him the message.

'Would you recognize either voice again?' Roger had asked, and was told that the manager 'thought he might', which was quite useless as far as evidence went.

There were messages waiting for him at the Yard, one from Gardener, saying that he had left *Poplars* at half past seven that morning, in a Newbury police car, in the wake of Andrew Kelham. Alexander was still at the house, which was being watched by Mellor. There was nothing else of importance, and he went along to make his report to Chatworth.

'Look here, West,' said Chatworth when Roger had finished his story, 'if you think your wife would be happier I'll give the case to someone else.' He grinned suddenly when he saw Roger's expression. 'All right, all right, don't look as if I'd accused you of treachery! Now, what about this Griselda woman? These people seem to be very worried about her.'

'Seem to be is right, sir,' said Roger. 'It might be a trick to make us concentrate on her while they get busy on something else.'

The telephone bell rang, and Roger turned to leave.

'Wait a minute, West!' said Chatworth. Roger turned back to see the AC listening intently to what was being said on the telephone. 'All right!' he said abruptly and rang off.

Then he looked at Roger. 'That was Sloan,' he said. 'He thinks he's cornered Griselda Fayne.'

CHAPTER TWELVE

The Finding of Griselda

DETECTIVE-INSPECTOR SLOAN, a tall, fresh-faced and powerful man whose fair hair was brushed flat and whose blue eyes held a look of excitement which reminded Roger of Gardener, was standing at the corner of a small street near Ealing Common. At the far end of the street were two other policemen in plain clothes, and there were several uniformed men within sight. Roger's car drew up at the corner, but did not turn into the street, and Sloan came hurrying forward.

'Is she still here?' asked Roger, eagerly.

'Yes, we've got her all right,' said Sloan, jubilantly. 'Spotted her myself, and followed her here. Recognized her and her clothes from the photograph and description you had circulated.'

'Is there anyone with her?'

'I don't know. No one else has been seen to enter or leave the house, but I haven't been much closer than this – I thought I'd better wait for you,' added Sloan, with a grin.

They walked quickly along the narrrow street with one sergeant following them and the other policemen watching closely. There were a dozen houses, small, detached and identical, each in a garden which was trim and neat, even that of *The Nook*, where Griselda Fayne had been seen to enter. Roger opened the gate. It squeaked. The double gates of the short drive-in to the garage were at the other side of the garden and the garage was out of sight.

The sergeant went round to the back, and Roger knocked at the door. There was no answer.

He knocked again, then pressed the bell. They heard it ring clearly, but after he took his finger off the bell-push there was only silence. Sloan coughed, and Roger frowned as he said:

'See if any of the windows are open, will you?'

The warrant he had brought gave him full authority to force an entry, and when Sloan came back to report that all the windows were closed and the back door was locked, Roger lost no time. He took an automatic from his pocket and broke the glass of the door with the butt. The pieces fell to the floor on the other side; there was no other sound.

Roger inserted his hand, and pulled back the knob. They stepped into a narrow, well lighted hall, which contained a hall wardrobe, one or two oddments of small furniture, and thick multi-coloured wool rugs on a polished wood floor. There were three doors in sight, and a staircase immediately in front of them.

'Will you go through and open the back door?' asked Roger.

When Sloan came back, Roger had looked through all the downstairs rooms, and found them empty. The furniture was modern and looked well kept, and there were two ash-trays with cigarette-butts, two or three of them with smears of lipstick. They went upstairs. There were four bedrooms and a bathroom, and all were empty. All had the same look as the room downstairs – as if they were regularly used and well kept.. The only sounds came from their own movements and low-pitched voices.

On the landing a chair was standing near the wall, immediately beneath the loft trap-door. Sloan stood by, watching anxiously, while Roger mounted the chair and pushed his hands against the loft door.

It fell back with a crash.

Roger gripped the side of the frame and hauled himself up. As he reached the boarded floor of the loft, he thought he saw something move, but when he straightened up – there was just enough room for him to stand upright – no one was in sight. Sloan came up quickly, and they stood together, looking round a surprisingly clean apartment. Suitcases and trunks were piled up in one corner with odds and ends of furniture and some pillows and blankets. In another corner water gurgled in a cistern. The loft was well lighted from a skylight, and was also fitted up with electricity.

Roger was looking towards the cistern, and suddenly he went down on his hands and knees. The cistern stood on wooden blocks which kept it clear of the floor, and left a gap of several inches. On the other side of the gap he saw a pair of shoes. He smiled faintly, and straightened up.

'All right, Miss Fayne,' he said. 'You can come out.'

He stepped towards one side of the cistern, and Sloan towards the other. There was a flurry of movement, and Griselda Fayne came into sight. All he saw at first were her bright eyes and the heavy walking-stick which she raised swiftly as she cried:

'Stand away! Stand away, or—'

Roger advanced as if she had not spoken. She swung the stick, but he put out an arm and brushed it aside. The next moment he had gripped her waist and she was standing and staring at him in mute defiance. In that moment, which should have been one of triumph, his chief emotion was pity for the girl. She looked on the point of tears.

'I knew I was right,' said Sloan, jubilantly.

Roger said: 'Will you be sensible?'

She said, bitterly: 'What else can I do?'

'That's the spirit!' said Roger. 'Go down, Bill, and give her a hand, will you?'

Griselda made no effort to break away. Sloan climbed through the hole and dropped, then Griselda followed him, going backwards, and Sloan stretched up and gripped her waist, then lowered her to the floor. A moment later Roger joined them, dusted his hands on his trousers, and said to the sergeant:

'Go and bring my car up here, will you?'

She said: 'How did you know I was here?'

'You were seen to come.'

'When?' asked Griselda, frowning. 'It was dark when I arrived.'

'Now look here,' said Sloan. 'I saw you come into this house this morning, not two hours ago, and—'

'Nonsense! I haven't been out of the house for twenty-four hours!' snapped Griselda.

'Oh,' said Sloan.

'You'd be a lot wiser if you looked for the others,' said Griselda, bitterly, 'instead of spending so much time looking for me. I can see that you don't believe me, but I haven't been outside the house for twenty-four hours. I know that someone else came here, another woman. There were some men here, too. I've been hiding in the loft, and I don't think they knew I was here. I tried to get down, but the bolt was pushed home.' She looked distraught, and her eyes were bloodshot and red-rimmed.

Sloan looked sceptical, but Roger said:

'When did you last have a meal, Miss Fayne?'

'At breakfast, yesterday.'

'Yesterday!'

'I had a small slab of chocolate, and it kept me going,' said Griselda, and then suddenly her voice broke, and she turned her face away and said in a muffled tone: 'I'm terribly thirsty. I – *could* I have a cup of tea?'

'You certainly can,' said Roger. 'Come into the kitchen.'

'There isn't much to tell,' said Griselda, when she had drunk the tea Roger prepared. 'I went to a friend's house and stayed there the night, and then I came here before it was light, yesterday morning.'

'Why did you come here?'

'I've done some work here, and I thought—' she broke off.

'Go on,' said Roger.

'I thought the people who lived here might help me,' said Griselda, and then she added fiercely: 'They killed Anthony Kelham! I practically heard them say so! You won't believe me, but they killed him.'

'How did you get in?' asked Roger.

'No one was up when I arrived, and I knew where they kept a back-door key,' said Griselda. 'It's in the garage. I was going to wait for them to come downstairs, when someone rang at the front door. I was in the kitchen – here – with the door open. I saw Mr Bellew open the door, and then I heard my name mentioned. A man came in and said that I'd been followed to Ealing, and had I turned up here. Bellew said "no". The man said that they had better be careful or they'd take the rap for the Kelham murder.' She was speaking very quickly, and her bright eyes were fixed on Roger. 'This *is* true,' she said, distressed, 'I know it sounds fantastic, but it *is* true.'

'What happened then?'

'They both went upstairs,' said Griselda. 'I suppose I should have left them, but I knew that you suspected me of the murder and I thought I might find out something else, so I stayed. I know the house well, you see. I went into the front room where there is a big screen, and stood behind it, in case they came in. There was Guy Bellew and his brother, and the stranger. They went into the kitchen, and I went upstairs. I thought the best place to hide was the loft. I thought that if they went out I could look through the house, and perhaps find some evidence. I hadn't been upstairs five minutes before they came up again. I was afraid they'd heard the loft-door close, but they didn't say anything. The chair is always in position beneath the loft, and there was nothing strange about it being there. So I stayed, listening to every sound, hoping they would go out. When they did, I tried to get down – but the loft door was bolted.'

Sloan was no longer looking sceptical. Both he and Roger were used to fantastic and improbable stories, and they were good judges of a liar. This story, with its wealth of detail, was somehow convincing.

Roger asked: 'Did these Bellew people go out yesterday?'

'They were out most of the afternoon, came back about seven o'clock, and went out again soon afterwards,' said Griselda. 'I heard them come in about one o'clock – it might have been later. I spread some pillows and blankets on the floor and tried to get to sleep. After what I'd heard, I knew it would be useless to let them know that I was here, you see. I – I had the idea that they were going to make you think that *I* had killed Anthony Kelham.'

'I see,' said Roger. 'Now about the Bellews. Is one of them a bald-headed, rather friendly-looking man?'

She stared, astonished. 'Yes, that's Mortimer!'

'And the other a tall, lantern-jawed fellow?'

'That's Guy!'

'And was the man who called here just after you a thick-set, rather ugly fellow with a grating voice?'

'Why yes,' said Griselda, faintly. 'So you know them?'

'I didn't know any of their names until you told me,' said Roger, 'but I've come across them before. When you first got to the loft, Miss Fayne, did you hear anyone immediately beneath the door?'

'Well, someone came upstairs, as I told you. I don't know where he stood. Why?'

Roger said: 'Because they doubtless knew you were in the house, guessed where you had gone, and shot the bolt to make sure that you were locked in.' He grinned at Sloan. 'It was neat, Bill, and they took you in, didn't they? They must have gone over the garden wall and out through some other front gate!'

Sloan said: 'I was watching and I never saw them

go. But I could have sworn the woman who came here this morning was you, Miss Fayne. She was wearing the clothes which fitted your description. The coloured mackintosh you mentioned,' he added to Roger, 'with a hood.'

'I left that at the hostel!' exclaimed Griselda.

'We can soon find out whether it's there,' said Roger.

The telephone was on the window-ledge. He called the hostel in Buckingham Palace Gate, and recognized the voice of the matron. No sooner had he given his name before she exclaimed:

'Inspector, you must come here at once! I have already reported to Scotland Yard. There has been a burglary here! Miss Fayne's room has been turned inside out! Most of her clothes are missing.'

'Is Miss Fayne's coloured mackintosh there?'

'*None* of her street clothes are here!'

'Not there, eh? That's good!' said Roger, and heard the matron gasp. 'I'll be along!' He rang off.

'But I can't see the sense of it,' said Griselda, helplessly. 'Why on earth—'

'You can't expect me to go into many details,' said Roger, reasonably, 'but here's a theory. Supposing they wanted to frame you, as you've said, and also wanted the police to find you? How could they do it better than to lock you in the loft, then let someone come here who would be recognized by the police, and get away themselves unobserved? Mind you, I don't say that is what happened, but it's possible.'

The sergeant who had brought his car to the house came back, and Roger and Sloan went into the small, pleasant back garden.

They easily spotted the gap in the fence through which the Bellews must have slipped, though it was hidden from the house by a corner of the brick-built garage that occupied part of the garden.

Suddenly the half-darkness inside the garage was illuminated by a vivid yellow flash. From inside came a roar, and Sloan gasped. Roger caught a glimpse of his head as he staggered backwards, and then Sloan pitched forward. The roar of a second revolver shot sounded deafening.

CHAPTER THIRTEEN

Smoked Out

'DROP THAT GUN!' snapped Roger and at the same moment he pulled his own automatic from his pocket and got out of range behind a corner of the garage.

Griselda was coming from the house with the sergeant and two more policemen. He beckoned them, and they reached him quickly.

'There's at least one and perhaps two armed men inside,' said Roger carefully. 'Keep your distance, and fire to wound, not to kill.' He handed the sergeant his gun, and added: 'Miss Fayne, you'd better get back to the house.' He looked at a constable. 'Go back with Miss Fayne, and telephone to Headquarters. Speak to the Assistant Commissioner personally, tell him that armed men are hiding in a garage here and that we may have to smoke them out. Tell him that Inspector Sloan has been wounded and we need an ambulance.'

When they had gone Roger surveyed the position more carefully. The neighbours on one side of *The Nook* were in the garden, but no one else seemed to have been disturbed. The two uniformed men were by the house and the sergeant and another two were close to the far end of the garage.

He reached *The Nook* end, and whispered to a policeman.

'Get some stones – those bricks will do – and throw 'em if necessary. Don't come any nearer.' He went cautiously towards the entrance where Sloan lay. He reached the

66

doorway and peered round. A dim electric light was burning. It cast the shadow of a man on the wall. He went a little nearer, and then he heard the familiar grating voice:

'Can't we take a chance?'

'Not yet, you fool – and keep an eye on the back door, damn you, or they'll come in that way!'

Roger thought that the man who moved towards the far end of the garage, and who carried a gun, was the tall man with the lantern jaw. He was quite sure of the identity of the man with the grating voice. He kept still for a moment, wishing that he had his own gun, then he took his hat from his head and held it out. A shot crashed out, and the hat was nearly shot out of his hand.

'Is that you, West?' the man called.

Roger said nothing, but gripped Sloan's feet and straightened his legs, then backed away a foot or two.

'Whoever it is, you'd better not come any farther,' the man said, 'you won't get out of here alive if you do.'

Roger remained silent, but pulled Sloan towards him. There was no more shooting, and he wondered if it meant that the men were short of ammunition.

'Look out, sir!' cried a policeman suddenly.

Roger jumped back. A bullet whined past, and the policeman hurled a brick into the doorway. It hit the wall at the far side. Roger looked round.

'Thanks, nice work. Watch him.'

He bent down again, and managed to get an arm beneath Sloan's chest and another under his legs. He grunted as he lifted the unconscious man. The second constable came hurrying to help him, and he hoisted Sloan over his shoulder and carried him towards the house. Griselda was watching from the kitchen window. In the lounge he put the man on a settee, and saw the two wounds in his chest. Sloan was pale, and his coat and waistcoat were wet with blood.

Griselda said: 'I will look after him.'

Roger was cheered by her confidence, and he hurried back to the scene of action. There had been no more shooting. The sergeant with his gun wanted to rush the garage, but Roger ordered him to do nothing of the kind. They would have to smoke the men out; there was no sense in risking their lives now, and it was only a matter of time – unless the trapped men decided to run for it, hoping to shoot a way through.

They now had plenty of spectators. People were standing in their gardens and at windows, ignoring brusque commands to go away. He took possession of his gun and stood at a point from which he could see both ends of the garage, so he would have good time to shoot if they made a sortie.

The tall man suddenly burst from the garage and rushed towards the top end of the garden, firing as he ran. The policeman in front of him ducked, and slipped. Roger fired and missed. Another policeman, ignoring the danger, plunged forward, a third threw a brick. The tall man raced on, firing twice again, and one of the bullets smashed the window of a house. Someone started to shout, and a woman screamed. Beyond the tall man were a dozen people, and if Roger fired again and missed he would probably hit one of them. He cursed the sightseers as he raced after the man. Roger gained on him, and then the man swung round and fired. Roger flung himself down. The bullet passed over his head, and now he was lying full length, and if he missed there was only a blank wall to hit.

He took careful aim, and the tall member of the Bellew family stopped in his tracks, and then pitched forward. The gun flew from his grasp.

The bullet had caught the man in the thigh, and it was the fall which had made him lose his gun. He was gasping for breath, and looked terrified.

Policemen came up, and Roger turned back to the garage, fearful now that the stocky man might have got away, but no one had seen anything more of him. As Roger was wondering whether he should risk his men's lives in a rush on the remaining man a car drew up outside the house, and men came hurrying from it. They were uniformed policemen, several of whom were carrying guns, and one of whom had a small canvas bag in his hand. It was an Ealing Division inspector whom he knew.

'We've got plenty of tear-gas,' he called as he came up. 'I hope we're not too late.'

'So do I,' said Roger. 'Let him have it!'

He wondered what the man inside was thinking as the brittle glass of the tear-gas 'bombs' broke against the floor of the garage, and the gas billowed about him. Roger, having no mask, had to stand by during the last stage, and he was on tenterhooks until, after what seemed an age, the thick-set man, coughing and spluttering and with tears streaming down his face, staggered out. The gas was spreading and Roger backed away, his eyes smarting. A gust of wind sent a cloud of gas towards the gardens where most of the sightseers were standing, and he grinned as they scattered.

He superintended the removal of the tall Bellew. The stocky man whose name he did not know was already in the kitchen, bathing his eyes. Men stood on either side of him, and the little house was full. Roger went through to see Sloan, and found him stripped to the waist, with cloth pads over the two bullet holes to stop the bleeding. He was still unconscious, but Griselda said:

'I think he'll be all right.'

He looked at the girl curiously. She still seemed tired, but she had done everything quickly and competently, at a time when she might have taken another opportunity to get away.

The ambulance arrived, and a police car from the Yard. From it stepped Chatworth's burly figure. He forced his way through a rapidly growing crowd of sightseers, and was hardly in the hall before he was yelling for Roger, who reported briefly.

'Hum!' said Chatworth. 'Let's see the rascal you caught.'

Roger led the way to the kitchen. The man was sitting dejectedly on a small chair, his eyes still watering, his chair wet and his clothes dusty and torn. He looked incapable of offering any more serious trouble.

'What's your name—' demanded Chatworth, who could

never be persuaded to leave questioning to his men if he were on the spot himself.

'What's yours?' retorted the prisoner.

'Now listen to me, my man, you—'

'Look out!' cried Roger.

He saw the knife which the man took from his pocket. A single leap, and the fellow was free of the policemen, who were taken completely off their guard. Roger went forward, and the man turned from Chatworth and, with the knife raised, leapt at him. He knew then that the fellow had allowed himself to be trapped and had waited for this moment, simply to get an opportunity of killing him.

CHAPTER FOURTEEN

The Man Who Would Not Talk

CHATWORTH swung his great arm, and as the knife touched Roger's chest, caught the man a blow on the side of the head which sent him flying sideways. Roger felt the point of the knife tear his waistcoat, and then heard it clatter to the floor. In a flash, two men were on his assailant, while Chatworth looked at his own hand, and then at Roger.

'Are you all right?'

'Thanks to you, sir, yes.'

'Dangerous customer,' said Chatworth. He did not ask why the man had not been searched; that would come later, and the policemen who had been watching him would not be let off lightly. 'Get him away as quickly as you can, and make sure he can't slip the handcuffs.' He watched as the handcuffs were put round the man's wrists, and, as he was being led to the kitchen door, he shot out a hand, grabbed his shoulder and swung him round. 'What's your name?' he demanded.

'Find out,' said the man, truculently.

'Damned impertinence,' fumed Chatworth.

It was twenty minutes before Roger had made all the arrangements. Men from the Ealing Division, with two from the Yard, were left at the house with instructions to make a thorough search. Guy Bellew was on the way to the Westminster Hospital, in the same ambulance as Sloan. Griselda Fayne was sitting in Roger's car, being eyed by fifty or sixty people who thronged the road, and the truculent prisoner was sitting in another car, with a policeman by his side and another at the wheel. Roger had a wash, dabbed his nose, which had started bleeding again, and had time to feel thankful that he had got off so lightly.

'I'll drive you back, sir, shall I?' he asked.

'Yes. Any particular reason why the girl should drive with us?'

'I think we'll find her amenable now, sir,' said Roger.

An hour later they were in Chatworth's office. Roger said, formally:

'Miss Fayne, I have not charged you, you are not under arrest, and you are at liberty to refuse to answer any questions which I might put. I hope you won't refuse. You own a portable typewriter, a *Royal,* don't you?'

Griselda looked startled.

'Yes, I take it about with me on business sometimes.'

'Have you ever typed anonymous letters on it?'

'Certainly not! Why should I?'

'You don't like Andrew Kelham,' said Roger, 'and he and the Assistant Commissioner here have received anonymous letters typed on your machine.'

'*I* didn't type them,' said Griselda.

'Do you ever lend the machine to anyone else?'

'I have done, but not lately. I suppose—' she broke off, and bit her lip.

'You were going to suggest that it could have been used at your room, in your absence,' said Roger.

'Well, it could, because the *Royal* is often there, I don't use it much. But I don't want to get anyone into trouble. I mean – well, who *could* have done it? I know all the girls

71

at the hostel, but I don't think any of them ever heard of Kelham.'

'I see,' said Roger. 'Now, what about the Bellews. How long have you known them?'

'For seven or eight years,' said Griselda, 'ever since I started work.'

'What work do you do for them?'

'The same as for everyone else. They don't have enough work to employ a full-time secretary, and they answered an advertisement of mine.'

'Did the advertisement have your name on it?' asked Roger.

'I suppose so.'

'Thank you,' said Roger. 'Have you ever had any idea that the Bellews were criminals?'

'I certainly have not! I always thought they were very decent people. They lived alone at Ealing, as far as I knew, and did everything themselves. I often went out to their house to work. They were – well, I liked then.' She sounded genuinely bewildered.

'What was their business?'

'Well, that's hard to define,' said Griselda. 'They dabbled in a lot of things – bought all kinds of different goods if they were going cheap, and sold them at a profit. Then they let and sold houses, and dealt in land.'

'Did they deal extensively in land or anything else?' he asked.

'Not really. It was a bit of this and a bit of that. They did most of their correspondence themselves, and kept all their own records. Most of the work I did was typing contracts and agreements, and writing sales letters.'

'Do you know the names of all their clients?'

'No, but I could probably remember a lot of them, if I put my mind to it.'

'That's one thing we'll want you to do,' said Roger. 'Among their visitors, was there anyone whom you would call remarkable?'

She hesitated, for the first time.

'Well – yes, I suppose there was. I didn't see many of

their callers, they used a little office in the City for interviews – it wasn't their office, but they had a share in it. The one man in any way remarkable was the fat man you saw the other evening.'

'Mr Kenneth Alexander,' murmured Roger.

'Yes. Have you seen him since?'

'Once. He called you his niece.'

Griselda made a face. 'He always did. The man is a beast! I've done work for him from time to time, and he was one of my best clients until about six months ago, when he overstepped the mark, and I stopped visiting him.'

'Where did you visit him?' asked Roger.

'In his flat in Putney. 22 Crane Court,' she added, as Roger held a pencil poised over a pad. 'Until last night I hadn't seen him for six months.'

'Why did you run away from him?'

'I didn't – I ran away from you!'

Roger smiled. 'He timed his visit, knowing you were there, and gave me the impression that he had come to get you away. Do you know why?'

'I haven't the faintest idea,' said Griselda.

'I see. Was he a friend of Andrew Kelham's?'

'Not to my knowledge,' said Griselda.

'You've never seen him at Kelham's flat?'

'No.'

'Were the Bellews acquainted with Kelham?'

'They sold him some land in south London,' said Griselda, 'but as far as I know they didn't see him personally. I wrote the letters and prepared the agreement.'

'Did you work for Andrew Kelham?'

'Sometimes.' She coloured. 'I did some work for him, because I hoped that I would find out something which would prove what a blackguard he is! But I've never found anything against him. If I didn't know what he had done to my father, I should have been completely deceived! He is such a two-faced hypocrite!'

Roger said suddenly: 'Why did you go to see Anthony Kelham on the evening of his murder?'

Her colour ebbed, and she put a hand to her breast.

Chatworth sat quite still, staring at her.

Then she said: 'I went to try to get some letters from him. Love letters. Andrew Kelham is bad enough, but his son was far worse. The letters weren't mine. They were written by a friend of mine to whom I introduced him. She is married. He laughed at me, we quarrelled, and I went out. I knew that Iris – my friend,' she amended hastily, 'was desperately anxious to get those letters. I imagined her despair if I told her I had failed, so I went back to try again. I found him dead.' She drew in her breath, and went on slowly. 'I looked in his pockets. The letters were there and I took them away. I'll never stop thanking God that I had the presence of mind to do that.'

It was not until the girl had been taken back to the waiting-room that Chatworth made a comment. He was thoughtful, and looked a little reluctant as he said:

'That gives us another motive against her.'

'This friend's husband might have known about them, and chosen to deal with young Kelham himself,' suggested Roger.

'H'm, yes. That would upset your pet theory about him being killed in mistake for his father, wouldn't it?'

'Theories are made to be upset,' said Roger, practically. 'I think it would be safer for her if she were detained on a minor charge, and I think she would understand that if we put it to her. We mustn't lose sight of the possibility, either, that she is hoodwinking us.'

Roger explained his idea to Griselda and then told a sergeant to lodge her in a 'cell' which was really a plainly furnished room kept for privileged prisoners, before he went to interview the thick-set man. At the start he did better than he expected for the man had already admitted that his name was Newman, after letters addressed to him at the Ealing house had been found in his pockets. When Roger entered his cell, however, he was obstinately silent.

Roger spent three-quarters of an hour trying, and

eventually gave it up as hopeless; the man knew that Sloan might die and that he might be charged with murder, but nothing would make him speak.

Roger went to the Ballistics Room. There, bullets fired from the guns taken from Bellew and Newman were compared with that taken out of Anthony Kelham's body. Roger hardly knew why he was not disappointed when the ballistics expert shrugged his shoulders, and said:

'You might have the men, but you haven't got the gun.'

He went back to his office, telephoned the hospital and was told that Sloan was still in the operating theatre. For a while he sat staring moodily at his desk.

Eddie Day came sailing into the office, and started when he saw Roger.

'Do you happen to know if anyone has been to the Royal White Hostel?' Roger asked him.

'Some woman was on the telephone just before you came in,' said Eddie. 'She asked for you, and she didn't half sound in a temper. I told her you'd ring her back.'

'I'd forgotten about her,' said Roger. 'I'll go and see her right away, tell her that if she comes through again, will you?'

Roger collected a plainclothes man and drove to Buckingham Palace Gate. The fact that he troubled to take a man with him when he knew there were already two watching the place was an indication of his frame of mind. He saw one of his men near the hostel, and pulled up near him.

'I've just telephoned a message for you, sir, about someone who's just gone in,' said the man. 'I think it's the fat fellow, Alexander, by his description. He's been in there about a quarter of an hour.'

The door of the hostel was opened by a short, rather dumpy girl. She was smartly dressed, and greeted him with a wide smile.

'I think the matron wants to see me,' said Roger. 'I'm from Scotland Yard.'

'Oh, yes. She *is* anxious,' said the girl. 'She's engaged at the moment, but I'm sure that she won't keep you long.'

'Who is with her?' asked Roger.

'The guardian of one of our girls,' she said, brightly. 'We have to assure them that everything is *very* proper here, of course.' The girl gave a laugh which was almost a giggle, but still Roger was unsuspecting. She led the way to a door marked: *'Visitors' Room'* and flung it open. 'I'll be back in a moment,' she added, and Roger stepped forward.

She pushed him in the back, and he nearly fell. Then she slammed the door, and Roger saw the gigantic figure of Mr Alexander standing behind the door and covering him with a small automatic.

'I'm *so* glad you've come,' said Mr Alexander.

CHAPTER FIFTEEN

Mr Alexander Discourses

'IN FACT," said Alexander, in a subdued voice, 'I felt quite sure that you would come when I was seen to come here. I watched your man hurrying to the telephone, and I must congratulate you on the promptness of your arrival, Inspector. You are most efficient. I could not talk freely in front of my good friend Andy Kelham, and yet I was so anxious to talk to you, Inspector.'

'You'd better be careful,' said Roger, 'or you'll have a heart attack.'

Alexander beamed.

'My dear Inspector, what a shrewd thrust! So you suspected the genuineness of my heart attack – ha-ha! A little capsule of adrenalin as I came down the stairs. Most effective! Now, Inspector, we must not waste time. My late dispatches from the battle-front, as one might say, suggest that you have seen quite enough shooting for one day, and

I am sure that you won't take any risks. Now, Inspector, I will come to the point. When you visited this hostel yesterday morning, you took some papers away.'

'They were afterwards taken from me,' said Roger.

'So I understand. Newman was very quick, I believe. I engaged him to obtain those papers for me, although I must dissociate myself from the methods which he employed. He is a violent, untrustworthy fellow, and I advise you to watch him most closely. I believe that he has exceptional strength in his hands, and has been known to strangle a fellow human being.' Mr Alexander shivered delicately. 'I duly received the papers and, to my great sorrow, paid for them in cash. They cost me fifty pounds, Inspector, and I found myself – cheated! The particular paper, which I know was in the possession of Griselda Fayne, was not among those I received. Newman gave me his solemn assurance that they were *all* he took from you, so *you* must still have the paper I want, Inspector.'

'Must I?' asked Roger, indifferently.

Alexander said: 'Inspector West, I want you to understand me *very* clearly. The idea about your child was mine, and I hope you appreciate the *finesse*. I gave strict instructions – by telephone, while my dear friend Andy was consoling his wife – that the child must not be harmed *at first*. I hope my instructions were carried out.'

'They were – and the men who carried them out aren't your strength now,' said Roger.

'Has it never occurred to you, Inspector, that human beings are the most easily replaced of creatures?' Alexander beamed. 'Let us return to the subject in which I am most interested – those papers. Have you taken them to Scotland Yard?'

'You'd better employ some more human beings to find out,' said Roger, calmly.

'Is it possible that you did *not* get them?' asked Alexander, as if speaking to himself. 'I wonder if Griselda has been smart enough to outwit me? She is a curious creature – yes – she might have had the wit to understand what was happening, and to have retained those particular papers. If so'

– he drew in his breath – 'what a distressing mistake has been made!'

'You should have questioned her before you let me arrest her,' said Roger.

'Possibly, possibly! Really, Inspector, you have made me feel quite weak.' He looked pale, and ran his hand across his forehead. 'To think that I might have been able to take them from Griselda – it appals me! I – stay there, Inspector! Don't move! I am watching you!'

Roger, who had straightened up, saw the fat fingers tighten about the gun, and stayed where he was. Yet he thought that for once Alexander was showing his true feelings.

'Dear me!' said Alexander, and raised his voice. 'Ethel!'

Obviously the girl had been standing outside the door, for she came in immediately. This must have been the girl who impersonated Griselda.

'Ethel,' said Alexander, in a low-pitched voice, 'there is reason to believe that Griselda had those papers, after all.'

The girl said viciously: 'That little—'

'Hush! The fault was ours, and we must admit it. Is Griselda under arrest, Inspector?'

'Yes,' said Roger.

'I see. Well, there is nothing else for it. You must send for her, West.'

'Oh yes,' said Roger. 'I'll send a postcard.'

Alexander took a step forward, his left hand raised, as if he were going to use violence. 'Now, understand me. You will make arrangements to get Griselda out of custody and to bring her here You have men outside – you can call to them from the window. Ethel – open the window! Now, West, do as I say. I'll kill you, if necessary!'

The girl unfastened the catch, drew aside the net curtain and began to push the window up. Roger glanced towards it, and Alexander motioned him forward with the gun. The man's eyes were narrowed and the gun was pointing towards his chest. It was impossible to see it from outside.

The window was wide open now, and the girl stood aside. Roger threw one glance at the amazing fat man, and then took his hand out of his pocket, holding a handful of silver and copper. He stepped towards the window. Suddenly he flung the coins over his shoulder, and made a rush for the window. The girl backed away in alarm. Roger vaulted through as the coins clattered about the floor. He held his breath, expected a shot and the shock of a bullet in his body. Then he dropped into the area of the semi-basement house, where his head was below the level of the window-sill.

The two men outside stared towards the window as Roger landed on his feet, but could not keep his balance. He went sprawling, and expected Alexander to lean out of the window and shoot him. He scrambled to his feet and pressed close against the wall. He was too breathless to call out, and he could not see his men. He heard a muttered exclamation from the girl, and then to his relief, the window was closed with a bang.

The two men came running towards the gate.

'Careful!' cried Roger. 'Careful!'

Then the front door opened and down the steps, with magnificent disdain, came Alexander. The girl was just behind him. Alexander reached the gate almost simultaneously with the policemen, and simply ran into them, striking out with both arms. He sent one man to the pavement and the other reeling back. Alexander even spared a moment to glance over his shoulder, and take Ethel's wrist. Then he led the way towards the nearest corner, dragging the girl after him. Neither of the policemen were steady enough to give chase, and Roger reached the gate before either of them started.

Alexander and Ethel disappeared round the corner.

When Roger reached it, he saw a car far down the road and knew that there was not the faintest hope of catching up with it. He stood breathing hard, until the others joined him, both looking scared when they saw his angry expression.

He went back to the house, taking one man with him. It

seemed deserted. In the first room beyond the one where the fantastic interview had taken place was a small telephone switchboard and a desk, but otherwise it was empty. Roger was sufficiently familiar with switchboards to put through a call to the Yard and to give warning that Alexander was in the Sloane Square and Victoria neighbourhood. Then he rang off, and was about to go farther along the passage when two girls appeared on the threshold.

'Who are you?' asked Roger, abruptly.

They stared at him in surprise, and one said:

'We live here. Who are you?'

'Inspector West of New Scotland Yard,' said Roger. 'I would like you to stay here, please, until I have finished.' He went along the passage, looking in all the rooms, but found them empty. Then he reached what was presumably the kitchen door; it was locked. He put his shoulder to it, but the door was too stout. He drew back, took a bunch of keys from his pocket and, selecting a skeleton key, began to pick the lock.

'Keep an eye on the stairs,' he said to his companion.

Then the door opened, and he stepped inside.

Three women stared at him, including the matron, whose hair was untidy and no longer in a bun at the back. The others were dressed in white overalls. They were sitting at a table, with scarves tied round their mouths and their arms bound to their sides. Another piece of rope tied them to their chairs.

As soon as he took the gag from the matron's mouth she began to complain, but he ignored her until he had freed the others, leaving her tied to the chair longest, as a reward for her caustic remarks.

At last he said sharply:

'How long have you been here?'

'For hours!' she exclaimed.

'That isn't true,' said Roger. 'Why make it worse by exaggeration?'

She looked as if she would start off again, but his expression stopped her, and she admitted that she thought they had been attacked about an hour before, but it might have been less. She had been giving instructions to the cook for the evening meal, and the maid had gone to open the door, admitting a *gross* creature who came in with one of the hostel's residents.

Roger's eyes brightened.

'The plump girl?'

'Yes, Ethel Downy. I *always* disliked that pert young woman!'

She went on and on; the fat man had held them up with a gun, and Ethel had bound them to the chairs. Roger gathered that Ethel had obtained a vindictive satisfaction out of it, and when he saw the red marks about the woman's wrists and neck, he was inclined to agree that she had suffered more than the others. The fat man and Ethel had locked them in, she said, and they had heard nothing more.

'I think you can call yourselves lucky that it was no worse,' said Roger. 'Now, I want full information about Ethel Downy, please. It's of great importance.'

The matron had collected her wits and she led the way to her study. There she opened a drawer in a steel filing cabinet, and took out a manila folder marked '*Downy, Ethel Mildred*'. There was a photograph, several letters of reference from previous landladies, and a brief list of particulars, for which Roger was grateful. Ethel Downy was an orphan whose parents had died many years before. She worked in the offices of the *Kelham Financial Trust*.

It was nearly eight o'clock before Roger reached the Bell Street house that evening, and it was pitch dark. A man moved towards him from outside the house, and shone a torch into his face. Then he backed away, and apologized.

'I didn't see it was you, sir.' It was one of the Yard men on guard at the house.

'That's all right,' said Roger.

A light was shining behind the curtains of the front room. As he opened the door, light streamed into the passage from the room, and Janet appeared.

'Oh, your poor nose!' she said. 'Supper's almost ready, I'll call you in five minutes.'

She went off to the kitchen, obviously seeing that he was in no mood to be taxed with questions, and he went into the front room and sat down in an easy chair, lit a cigarette, and looked moodily at Mark, who was sitting at the piano and resumed playing, softly.

He was surprised when, after ten minutes or so, Janet shook his shoulder.

'Wake up, sweet, or it will spoil.'

'I haven't been asleep,' said Roger, sitting up quickly.

He ate with relish and felt better when he had finished and they were drinking coffee in the front room. During supper Janet had told him that there had been no hint of trouble, that Mark had been there since the middle of the afternoon, anxious not to miss anything, that Pep Morgan's two men had been relieved at Mrs Norman's, and that the Yard men, also relieved, were *sweet*.

He gave them the story of the day's events. Neither of them interrupted, although Janet held her breath once or twice. She was sitting on a pouffe in front of a small log fire, and Mark was squatting on the piano stool.

'What about these missing papers? Does Griselda know anything about them?' asked Mark, when Roger's recital ended.

'She says not. I wish I were quite sure that she is altogether honest,' said Roger, frowning. 'I can't really make up my mind. Her refusal to give the name of her friend is peculiar. She should know that we would handle the business discreetly, and that the husband need know nothing about it. I can't help wondering whether he did know about it, and went and shot young Kelham. Griselda might even have seen him there – at the flats – just before or after, and it may explain why she got so worked up.'

At seven o'clock the next morning, the telephone bell disturbed him. Janet was already up. He groped for the telephone, on the bedside table.

'West,' he said gruffly.

The eager voice of Detective-Constable Gardener made him sit up; Gardener was watching Kelham and Blair at the Majestic Hotel.

'Is that you, Inspector? I say, I think Kelham's disappeared! His man, Blair – you know – is rushing about like a man demented. He says that Kelham's not in his room, and his bed hasn't been slept in. I've been within sight of the door all night, and *I* haven't seen him!'

'I'll come over at once,' said Roger.

Within twenty minutes he was out of the house and driving through the nearly deserted streets towards the Majestic, which was near Marble Arch. He was thinking evil thoughts of Gardener, but forbore any immediate reprimand when that eager young man greeted him on the landing near Kelham's room.

'That's the door – this side of the one where the maid's going in with tea,' said Gardener. 'I've been sitting here all night, and I *swear* I haven't dozed for a moment. I had a good sleep when I got back yesterday, and I was as fresh as a daisy, I was really, Inspector. I – Great Scott, what's that?'

He spoke to Roger's back, for Roger was racing along the passage towards the room into which the maid had disappeared. She was screaming wildly, and the morning tea-tray had crashed to the floor.

CHAPTER SIXTEEN

No Respite for Roger

WHEN ROGER turned into the room the maid had stopped screaming, but she was staring towards the bed and shivering from head to foot. On the bed lay Kelham.

He was fully dressed, and his face was covered with blood, his hair matted. One arm hung by the side of the bed, almost touching the floor.

Roger looked over his shoulder as Gardener came in.

'Get Dr Winter. Tell the messenger at once, and make sure this girl doesn't blab all over the hotel.'

'Right-ho,' said Gardener. 'Come along, my girl.' He led the maid out, while Roger, afraid that Kelham was dead and feeling a sickening sense of futility, bent over the man and felt his pulse.

His expression altered, for he could detect a faint beating. He straightened Kelham out on the bed and loosened his collar and tie. By that time he knew that the man was alive. He examined the head wounds. They were comparatively light, and the bone had not been broken. There was an ugly gash on one temple, which had caused most of the bleeding, but that was the worst feature. Roger propped him up on pillows, and decided that it would be better not to touch the wounds until the doctor arrived. He was washing his hands when Gardener came back with the agitated manager.

'Dr Winter's on his way, sir,' he reported, 'and I said we would want photographs and fingerprints. Was that all right, sir?'

'Yes, good,' grunted Roger, and spent a few minutes assuring the manager that he would not want the hotel roused, but did want to know who had engaged the room where Kelham was found, and would soon want to question the servants on that section. The manager grew calmer and promised all possible help.

'This is a do, isn't it?' said Gardener, when the man had gone. 'I knew I hadn't seen him come out. There's a communicating door, sir.'

It was not locked. Roger stepped through into the next room, which was almost identical with the one where Kelham had been found. That was empty, but there were two filing cabinets which had been brought from the flat, and several suitcases, as well as a cabin trunk. Kelham had obviously been prepared to stay away from the flat for some time. Brushes, shaving tackle and other oddments were neatly distributed about the room.

'Go and find Blair,' said Roger.

He was glad to be on his own. He did not try to theorize, but stood still, reviewing all that had happened, waiting for the doctor.

Dr Winter arrived, brisk and dispassionate, with little to say. He spent five minutes examining Kelham, and then looked up at Roger.

'He'll be all right in a week.'

'What caused the wounds, do you know?'

'It looks rather like broken china or glass,' said the police-surgeon. 'Nothing went deep. Better make a hospital case of him, hadn't we?'

Roger said thoughtfully: 'I think we'll take him to his flat. We've a couple of men there and they can do two things at the same time. He'll want a nurse, I suppose?'

'One ought to look in two or three times a day,' said the doctor, 'but he won't want much attention. Let me see – oh, yes, the flat in Park Lane. I'll go along with the ambulance, if it will help you.'

There was a telephone in the room, and Roger called the men at Kelham's flat and gave them precise instructions. He was relieved that Sergeant Willis was back on duty there.

Gardener came back, with a worried expression.

'I can't find Blair, sir.'

'Go downstairs to the reception desk and find out if he's been seen to leave,' said Roger, keeping his temper with an effort.

There were several exits from the mammoth hotel, and he thought it likely that Blair might have got away unnoticed. He lit a cigarette, scowling about him as the fingerprint men and the photographers arrived.

'Not much here, sir, the place has been wiped over pretty well,' said the fingerprint man regretfully, after a few minutes.

Roger went downstairs to see the manager. The room next to Kelham had been booked by a man calling himself

'Smith', and none of the staff remembered him well. The room had been booked two days before. By checking, Roger was able to establish that it had been reserved an hour after Kelham had taken residence – or rather, after Blair had made the reservation. The floor staff could only describe him as an ordinary little man, and it was in a moment of inspiration that Roger asked the chambermaid:

'Was he bald-headed?'

The chambermaid, who was not very bright, looked at him wide-eyed, and said:

'Well, what a funny thing, sir!'

'What's funny about being bald?' demanded Roger.

'Well, sir, he wasn't *bald*, but one morning he was asleep when I went in – I mean, yesterday morning, sir.' She gulped, and tried to overcome her nervousness. 'I thought his hair looked funny, sir, as if it were all on one side, if you know what I mean.'

'A wig!' exclaimed the manager.

Roger said: 'Wait here a minute, will you?' He went outside and asked the photographer whether he had in his bag any prints of people connected with the case. To his delight, the man produced photographs of the Bellews and Newman. 'You're handy with a pencil, aren't you?' asked Roger. 'Put some hair on the bald fellow, will you, and bring it into the manager's office.'

Ten minutes later, the chambermaid stared at the touched-up photograph, and gasped:

'Why, it's the spit image of him, sir!'

'Good,' said Roger. 'Did he have any visitors, do you know?'

'I didn't *see* any, sir.'

He could get no evidence that Mortimer Bellew, who was undoubtedly the man who called himself 'Smith', had received visitors, but he was fairly well satisfied with the results so far obtained. He put Gardener outside the door, got rid of the photographer and the fingerprint man, and then began a systematic search of the papers. After half an hour he began to feel tired of looking at copies of agreements and bills which he had seen before, but suddenly he exclaimed aloud.

He had found the agreement for the piece of land which the Bellews sold Kelham.

It seemed to be in order, but he set it aside, and started work again. One agreement caught his eye, but when he looked at it again he could not see what interested him, until he saw the address: it was a house in Buckingham Palace Gate.

'Well, I'm damned!' he exclaimed, and hurried to the door. 'Gardener, what number Buckingham Palace Gate is that girl's hostel?'

'21b, sir.'

The number of the plot which Kelham had bought was 101a. He set that agreement aside, and ran through the others. He found nothing else of interest and, realizing that he was ravenously hungry, arranged for some breakfast to be brought up to the room. It was then half-past ten.

He left Gardener to watch the rooms, and went along to the Yard. Before going to Chatworth's office, he looked through the messages on his desk. A messenger came in with an envelope.

Roger opened it. The memo inside was headed: *'Telephoned at 11.15 a.m.'*, and it went on to say briefly: *'From Det. Sergeant Mellor for Chief Inspector West. Charles Blair arrived at Poplars at 10.45. Instructions, please.'*

He telephoned the Newbury Police Station immediately and asked an inspector to send a message telling Mellor to detain Blair if he left the house, and then hurried along to see Chatworth. He was greeted by a scowl which made his heart sink.

'*Good* morning, Inspector,' said Chatworth, sitting back in his chair. He tapped a letter on his desk. 'I have a most emphatic complaint about your handling of matters at the hostel, Inspector. The matron, who signs herself Agatha Barton, complains that you were rude, impertinent and insolent, and accuses you of gross neglect of duty.'

'I was short with her,' said Roger, 'but I don't think she's justified in the other comments. She—'

'I see, I see,' Chatworth interrupted. He pulled at his underlip. 'Well, I'll send her a polite letter, and trust you to justify your actions by results as usual.'

'Thank you, sir. What I came to tell you about at the moment,' Roger went on, 'is that Charles Blair left the hotel, dodged our men' – he omitted to name Gardener – 'and went straight to Kelham's Newbury home. Mellor has just reported. I'd like to go down to Newbury, sir. Kelham probably kept papers there. Now we have an excuse for scrutinizing them, I think we ought to take it.'

'You'd better go,' said Chatworth.

Roger went home, picked up a packet of sandwiches, kissed Janet and Scoopy and then, accompanied by Mark Lessing, drove off.

The journey was uneventful, and they passed through Newbury and turned into the drive of *Poplars* a little after three o'clock. Mellor was standing near some bushes just inside the drive, and as they passed he cocked a thumb, meaning that everything was unchanged on that sector. Roger climbed out of the car and knocked at the door, leaving Mark in the car.

The maid who had answered his first call opened the door.

'Good afternoon, sir.'

'Good afternoon,' said Roger. 'I think Mr Blair is here.'

'He's with Mrs Kelham, sir.'

'Good! Tell him I want to see him, will you?' asked Roger, and when the maid had gone, he grinned back at Mark.

Blair came down the stairs quickly, his face set in a scowl.

'Well, what do you want now?' he demanded.

'You,' said Roger, 'and don't get fresh. You made yourself liable to arrest when you ran away from London, and don't make any mistake about it. Why did you hurry down here?'

'That's my business!'

'I see,' said Roger. 'So you're going to make me take a strong line, are you? I—'

'*Charles, dear!*' called a woman, in a gentle voice. '*Charles, who is it?*'

The voice had a curious quality of softness which made Rogert start, and he looked towards the landing. Blair half turned, with his hands clenched. A woman came along the passage to the head of the stairs. She wore a pale blue dressing-gown, her luxuriant grey hair was piled up, pompadour fashion, and she seemed to glide along. She was astonishingly lovely, and had a regal air as she descended the stairs.

CHAPTER SEVENTEEN

Mrs Andrew Kelham

BLAIR SPOKE out of the corner of his mouth in a voice which Roger only just heard.

'If you've got an atom of decency in your make-up, you won't tell her that Andy has been hurt. She can't stand a shock.' He went forward and held out his hand. 'Why, Lynda, how nice to see you downstairs again!' He took her arm and tucked it into his, and she accepted this with a childlike docility. 'This is Mr West, a friend of Andy's.'

'Good afternoon, Mr West,' said Mrs Kelham, with a gentle smile. 'I am very glad to see you. You must be a new friend of Andy's, because he hasn't mentioned you to me.'

'I am a business acquaintance,' murmured Roger.

'Oh, business! When *is* Andy going to allow himself to rest from it?' asked Mrs Kelham, frowning. There was a hint of reproof in her manner. 'Are you one of the people who will worry him so much, and won't allow him to spend a few weeks here, with me?'

'I had no idea that he was in need of a rest,' said Roger.

'I see.' She smiled, sweetly. 'Do forgive me for what I said, Mr West. I have been upset because Andy has been detained in London again, and may not be back here for a week or more. Charles has told me all about it; I am afraid no one has any influence over Andy, except that *noisome* Mr Alexander! He isn't here, is he?'

'I think he's in London,' said Roger.

'Are you one of his men?' demanded Lynda Kelham.

'Most decidedly not!' said Roger.

'I'm very glad,' said Lynda. 'I wish it were possible for me to forbid Alexander and all his friends entry to the house. I do not believe they exert a good influence. There are times when I think Mr Alexander is positively evil.'

'Lynda—' began Blair, in great distress.

'You may think that it is none of my business,' said Lynda, 'but I have held my peace too long. When Andy came here last he looked really ill, and I do not believe that it was because Anthony has been sent abroad. Andy is overtired, and unless he rests he will have a breakdown. Mr West' – she stretched out her hand, appealingly – 'can *you* persuade him to go more steadily?'

'I will gladly try,' said Roger, with an effort.

'How kind of you. Charles, isn't Mr West kind?' She smiled, and then leaned more heavily against Blair. 'Perhaps I will go upstairs again, Charles. I did not realize that it would take so much effort to come down. Goodbye, Mr West. Thank you for your promise. *Do* talk seriously to Andy as soon as you see him, won't you?'

She held out her hand; it was dry and hot.

Roger stood watching while Blair helped her up the stairs.

He had not dreamed that Kelham had lied to her about Tony, but he understood, now, why Kelham had been so anxious to come himself to 'break the news'.

He lit a cigarette, and had nearly smoked it before Blair came hurrying down the stairs.

'West, that was damned sporting of you! I'm really grateful, and I know Andy Kelham will be.'

'That's all right,' said Roger, slowly. 'Why did you come down here, Blair? Was it to tell her that Kelham had been detained and to prevent her from learning that he was injured?'

'Yes,' said Blair. 'That, and to make sure that no one else blabs out the truth. She mustn't have a shock of any kind. Tony has gone abroad. Later on, when she's stronger, she'll have to know the truth, of course, but it might be fatal if she were to learn it now.'

'I see,' said Roger. 'Why on earth didn't you or Kelham tell me about this before?'

'Andy was going to tell you this morning,' said Blair. He drew in his breath sharply. 'How is he?'

'Not badly hurt. He'll be all right in a week's time. Exactly what happened last night, Blair?'

'*I* don't know,' said Blair. 'I had a room next to his. He said he felt washed out and would have an early night, and asked me to call him at seven o'clock. When I went into his room it was empty and the bed hadn't been slept in. I – I rather lost my head, I'm afraid.'

'You did,' said Roger. 'Did Kelham have any visitors at the hotel?'

'Not to my knowledge.'

'Does he know two brothers, named Bellew?'

'Bellew?' repeated Blair, frowning. 'The name's familiar, but I don't think he knew anyone of that name well. He – oh, I remember. He bought one or two houses from them, not long ago. Why?'

'One of the Bellews attacked him,' said Roger.

Blair stared, incredulously.

'Why on earth—'

Roger said: 'Blair, I'm going to be frank with you and I hope you'll reply in kind.' He paused, and Blair looked harassed. 'The truth is that the Bellews believed themselves to have been tricked and cheated by Andrew Kelham,'

91

went on Roger, mendaciously, 'and they attacked him out of a spirit of revenge. On your own admission, you know most of Kelham's business. If I am to save him from further injury, and perhaps from death, I must know exactly what has been happening. Did he cheat the Bellews?'

'No, of course not!' said Blair angrily. 'If that's the yarn they've told you, you can ignore it. Andy Kelham treats everyone with the utmost fairness – no one has any possible cause for complaint against him.'

'Oh,' said Roger, his little scheme stillborn. He had hoped to frighten Blair into making some kind of admission, but instead he saw only a burning sincerity; Blair believed all that he said of his employer, although it was so different from Griselda's opinion. He went on, thoughtfully: 'I don't want to call you a liar, Blair, but others besides the Bellews have good reason to hate Kelham, including' – he paused, and then uttered the name with great deliberation – 'Griselda Fayne.'

'*What?*' cried Blair, and then went on quickly: 'Now look here, West, I don't know how you've got hold of this story, but you can take it from me that you're wrong. Griselda didn't like some of the things Andy did, but she had a great respect and admiration for Andy. Ask her yourself, and she'll tell you.'

Roger rubbed his chin.

'And really, there's no need to think that I can tell you more,' went on Blair. 'Why do you keep laying traps for me? Kelham was a great friend to Griselda, and wanted her to become one of the family – I've told you that before. If Anthony had been anything like him—' he broke off.

'So you didn't like his son,' said Roger, thoughtfully.

'No, I didn't!' snapped Blair. 'You can think it's because of Griselda if you wish. I had no personal grudge against him, except that I hated the thought that Griselda might marry him one day, but there were plenty of people who disliked Anthony Kelham!'

'You didn't tell me anything of this the other evening,' said Roger. 'In fact you gave me a very different impression.'

'Well, supposing I did?' said Blair. 'He's dead now, and I saw no point in raking up a lot of muck. It was bad enough for Andy as it was. I suppose I shouldn't have told you this,' he added. 'You've a motive against me, now. Not that I killed him,' he added, and Roger thought that he was rapidly becoming distraught. 'Nor did Griselda, she — where is she, West?'

'Under arrest,' said Roger.

'I suppose that was inevitable,' said Blair, 'but take my word for it, West, you've got to find someone else. Griselda didn't kill him.'

'We'll find out who did,' said Roger, taking out cigarettes. Blair accepted one. 'Now,' went on Roger, as he put his case away, 'what about this man Alexander?'

Blair said: 'He's a friend of Andy's.'

'Mrs Kelham thought he exerted an evil influence,' Roger reminded him.

'I know, but — well, she isn't quite herself, surely you saw that.'

'How well did you know him?'

'I've met him a number of times,' said Blair. 'I didn't have much time for him, but he's a very shrewd business man, there's no mistake about that, and Andy Kelham is first and last a business man. Look here, West, aren't we wasting time talking about Alexander?'

'I don't think so,' said Roger. 'When did you last see him?'

'Oh, weeks ago. At the Park Lane flat. What difference does that make?' Blair looked at his watch. 'Good Lord, it's nearly four o'clock! Will you have some tea? Excuse me!' He turned and hurried through the doorway leading to the domestic quarters, leaving Roger standing and staring after him.

From outside there came a short, sharp note on the horn of his car. He turned towards the door, opened it, and saw Mark standing by the car, looking both bored and aggrieved.

'Forgotten me?' asked Mark.

'No. You'd better come in.' As Mark joined him in the

porch, Roger went on: 'This is the queerest show. Mrs Kelham is beautiful and nearly simple. She doesn't know about the murder nor the attack on Kelham, and Blair looked murderous when he thought I was going to tell her. Mrs Kelham has a strong dislike of Alexander, by the way.'

'And who can blame her?' demanded Mark.

'I want to find out why,' said Roger. 'I'm going to take Blair away, and I'd like you to stay and try to find out why Alexander is so unpopular. I think you'll find that she's easy to handle. You'll win her sympathy if you say how much you admire her husband, how tired he is looking, and that you'll do all you can to persuade him to rest. Is that all clear?'

Blair raised no objection to going back to London, but insisted on obtaining a further assurance that Mrs Kelham would not be told the truth. Mark, declaring that he had friends in Newbury, left the car in the centre of the town, and Roger drove on in silence, with Blair at his side.

They had been driving for half an hour before Blair spoke.

'Who told you that Griselda didn't like Andy?'

Roger shot him a quick glance. 'She told me herself.'

'Oh,' said Blair. 'I – I suppose I'm not really surprised. West, do you seriously think that she shot Tony, thinking him to be his father?'

'I'm reserving judgement and trying not to form conclusions,' said Roger, 'and I am a policeman, and not at liberty to talk freely. I've been more frank with you than I should have been,' he added. 'I hope you'll remember that. I—'

He broke off, and stared at a small car which was being driven towards him. There was something familiar about it, and as it drew nearer, he thought he recognized the Morris car in which Newman and the Bellews had got away from Buckingham Palace Gate. The Morris passed, and he caught a glimpse of the driver, who was alone. It was Mortimer Bellew.

94

Roger suddenly accelerated and swung into a side turn-ing, sending Blair heavily against the door. Roger braked sharply, went into reverse, and backed into the main road, so that he could follow the little car. Blair was still recovering from the sudden jolt, and clutching the handle of the door.

The road ahead was empty; the little car had disappeared round a bend. Roger trod heavily on the accelerator, and in a few minutes caught a glimpse of his quarry driving along a tree-lined stretch of road. Had he chosen, he could have caught up with Mortimer Bellew, and he did not think he would have any difficulty in effecting an arrest, but he was chiefly anxious to find out where the man was going.

'What *has* come over you?' demanded Blair, aggrievedly.

'That's the fellow who attacked Kelham,' said Roger. 'I don't want you to interfere except in emergency.' He saw the car disappear round another bend and, remembering that there were cross-roads just ahead of it, accelerated again.

He swung round the corner.

'Look out!' cried Blair.

The Morris was pulled up in the middle of the road, and Mortimer Bellew was hurrying away from it, towards the hedge. Roger wrenched the wheel to the left, where there was more room than on the other side, but it was too late to avoid a crash. He trod on the brakes, but the collision came with a sickening jolt and he was flung forward against the wheel, all the breath knocked out of his body. His head struck the windscreen, but he did not lose consciousness. The little car was pushed several yards along the road, and the rending sound of bending metal and the screaming of locked brakes broke the quiet of the evening.

CHAPTER EIGHTEEN

Mr Alexander Again

DAZED AND gasping for breath, Roger straightened up. He saw Blair sprawled forward against the windscreen, unconscious. The glass had cracked but not splintered. The front of his car and the back of the little one were hopelessly intermingled. When he tried to open the door, he could not. He pushed at it wildly, without getting any result, and then leaned back and managed to open the back door.

At last he stumbled into the road, and stood upright, breathing deeply and feeling sore in every limb.

There was no sign of Bellew, and there was no other traffic. He thought that if a car came at any speed round the bend there would be an even worse crash, but it was impossible to move the cars on his own. He decided that it would be better to get to the corner and wave a warning rather than to try to get Blair out and risk a crash while they were both in danger. He had little doubt that Bellew knew he had been recognized, and had decided to get away on foot.

As he turned the corner, a man was hurrying along the road towards him, a roughly dressed countryman.

'I thought I heard a crash.'

'You did,' said Roger, 'and a nasty one. Will you stand here for ten minutes, and warn any cars which come along?'

'Why, yes, sir.' The man looked alarmed. 'Anyone hurt?'

'I hope not,' said Roger.

He hurried back to Blair, and was relieved to see that the man was recovering consciousness. The door on Blair's side opened without difficulty, and Roger helped him out. It suddenly occurred to him that he did not remember having passed the countryman on the road as he was driving. The nearest by-road was a mile or more back, and unless the man had walked across fields, he must have been waiting near there.

'I – I'm all right,' muttered Blair, leaning against the hedge. 'I'm – all right, I tell you.'

'Stay here for a couple of minutes,' said Roger.

As he spoke, he heard a car approaching, and heard the countryman call out.

Blair's right arm was hanging limply by his side; from the elbow downwards it seemed to be bent at a peculiar angle; he thought that it was broken.

'I think—' began Roger.

'Why, what a remarkable coincidence!' exclaimed a man from behind him. 'What an astonishingly small world it is, Inspector! My dear sir, how are you? Not hurt, I trust.'

Roger swung round, putting his hand to his pocket for his gun; but he did not get that far, for Alexander had a small automatic in his right hand, and was pointing it towards him. By Alexander's side was the countryman, grinning widely, and at the top of the hedge there appeared the rather startled face of Mortimer Bellew.

'Really, Inspector, you look quite vindictive!' said Alexander. 'In view of your remarkable escape, you should be feeling most grateful to the winds of chance! Bellew, stop looking like a frightened rabbit, and come down and help to move those cars!' Bellew climbed over the hedge, and Alexander went on: 'Not you, Inspector, you mustn't tire yourself, you really mustn't. Turn around.'

Slowly, helplessly, Roger turned round.

'Walk along the road and turn into the copse through the first gate,' said Alexander. 'I shall be close behind you, and if you show the slightest inclination to run, I shall shoot you without compunction.'

Roger walked on slowly. He had forgotten his aches and pains in the new danger. The temptation to break into a run was almost overwhelming, but he kept on a steady course and reached the gate, which led into a thick copse.

Just in sight beyond the copse, only its roof visible because it was in a dip in the ground, was a farm-house. As he drew nearer he saw the cluster of outbuildings about it.

The man leading the way stopped at the front door of the stone-built farm-house.

'Go inside, West,' said Alexander. 'Upstairs.'

The wide, stone-flagged hall was gloomy and dark. The stairs were wide and the treads shallow. There was a bend halfway up them, and Roger, glancing over the side, weighed up the chances of jumping over the banisters and getting behind Alexander. At last they reached a door which the man in front opened. Roger went in.

The room was furnished in such a fashion that, in spite of the oppressing thought on his mind, Roger was startled. It might have been lifted out of a London flat. The furniture was expensive, there was a thick carpet, and the walls were painted a deep yellow. Books lined one of the walls, near the wide, leaded-paned windows. The whole room gave an impression of luxury and culture which he somehow failed to associate with Alexander, who followed him into the room, and said:

'Sit down in that chair by the bureau.'

Roger sat down. Alexander stepped to the window, still keeping his gun in his hand. The door remained open, and one of Alexander's men stood outside it, watchfully.

'Now, West,' said Alexander, 'we have had more than enough of this folly. I could have shot you dead at the hostel. I could have shot you in the road. I have had ample opportunity to kill you, but I have no wish to commit murder unnecessarily. Moreover, you can be of assistance to me. West, it is necessary for me to talk with Griselda Fayne. I do not think that it will be necessary for me to injure her, and I am prepared to give you my word that at the end of twenty-four hours she will be returned to you unharmed. I will make a further offer to you, West. You want the murderer of Anthony Kelham. I will name the murderer and give you all the evidence you need for a conviction, and I will also help you to clear up the whole mystery. Now that Kelham is dead, it will not matter.'

Roger hoped that he had not shown the surprise which ran through him. Only a few hours before he had been astonished at Mrs Kelham's ignorance about the death of her son, but that was insignificant compared with Alexander's belief that Kelham was dead.

Roger said: 'How do you expect me to arrange it?'

'It will be quite simple. If you telephone Scotland Yard – there is a telephone in front of you – and arrange for one or two of your men to bring Griselda to Kelham's house at Newbury, no one will question your instructions. I know that you are held in high regard at Scotland Yard, and the very fact that she is to have an escort will kill suspicion. When she is on the way there, I will apprehend her. I have done it with you; I can do it with her.'

'Supposing I refuse?' asked Roger.

Alexander said: 'I shall kill you out of hand. Make no mistake about it.' He paused, and then added heavily: 'West, lift up the blotting-pad in front of you.' When Roger stared at him, he added harshly: 'Lift it up!'

Slowly, Roger moved the pad.

He winced at what he saw. There was a snapshot of Janet and Martin taken recently, the child in his mother's arms. It must have been stolen from Bell Street.

Roger looked up at him.

His face was set. The hatred he felt for this man showed in his eyes, hiding his agony of mind. Alexander opened his mouth to speak again, but uttered no word as he returned Roger's gaze. The room was very quiet, but outside the clatter of the tractor-driven plough shattered the quiet of the afternoon, and seemed to hammer into Roger's brain.

'I will telephone my office,' Roger said.

CHAPTER NINETEEN

Sir Guy Chatworth's Opinion

HE SPOKE to the operator at Scotland Yard in a harsh clipped voice.

'This is Chief Inspector West. Put me through to the Assistant Commissioner at once, please.'

'Hold on, sir.'

'Would not one of the other men do?' asked Alexander, in a penetrating whisper.

Roger looked up at him. 'No,' he said, and looked back at the telephone and the photograph of Janet which was now resting against it. He felt physically cold and numbed. He saw no alternative to this abject surrender, but the arguments for and against no longer occupied his mind. He was very close to despair; the whole code of his life was wrecked, he had never faced so great a crisis. All thought had left him except the awful, all-pervading realization that he had failed both himself and his colleagues. He knew that the photograph had tipped the scales; without it he would have risked defiance.

There were sundry noises on the telephone, and Roger could hear snatches of a distant conversation. He wondered if he had been cut off, and then, in the midst of his thoughts, came Chatworth's hearty voice.

'Hallo, West, where are you speaking from?'

'Newbury, sir,' said Roger. '—I—'

'Speak up, man! What's the matter with you, West? You don't sound a bit like yourself.'

'I don't sound a bit like myself', thought Roger, and his grip tightened on the telephone. Alexander could not know that Chatworth was already puzzled. For the first time he felt a surge of hope, and he had to fight against revealing that in his voice.

'I don't want to be overheard,' he said. 'I have just come

from Andrew Kelham's house and there is likely to be trouble there unless I get back quickly. I can handle it all right, though. I think I'm very near the end of it, sir.'

Alexander loomed over him, tight-lipped; this was not the conversation which he had expected.

'Do you?' asked Chatworth, and he still sounded puzzled.

'Yes, sir. I shall be able to find out for certain when I have had a talk with Griselda Fayne. I think the best thing would be to send her down here, under escort. She *must* take the Reading–Newbury road. Will you arrange that, sir?'

'You're being very mysterious,' said Chatworth.

'I would explain more fully if I had the time,' said Roger, 'but I haven't a moment to spare. Will you do it?'

'Oh, all right,' growled Chatworth.

'Thank you, sir. I will report again just as soon as I can,' said Roger. 'Goodbye.'

He replaced the receiver, and sat staring in front of him. In the photograph the curve of Janet's lips seemed to grow deeper, and he had an absurd fancy that the child smiled. His forehead was beaded with sweat and the palms of his hands were moist. The bleakness of the first few minutes was passing, and he no longer felt the same overwhelming sense of shame. Chatworth *might* read between the lines of that conversation, might take some steps to prevent the worst from happening. He saw a possibility, a vague one perhaps, but nevertheless there, of finding out why Alexander wanted to talk to Griselda so urgently.

Sir Guy Chatworth prided himself that he knew his men thoroughly. He had a high opinion of Roger West, and had come to the conclusion that Roger's recent show of short temper had been excusable and that his own attitude could not have been better calculated to anger him. Roger was labouring under a great strain, and the threat to his wife and child increased it. Because of that, Chatworth had prepared himself to be most amiable when Roger was put through on the telephone, but when he replaced the receiver he sat staring at it thoughtfully.

'Now I wonder what his trouble is,' he mused. 'He certainly didn't sound himself. What did he say, now? she *must* take the Reading–Newbury road. Now that is peculiar, most peculiar. If he wants to see her at Kelham's house, what difference does it make which road she takes?' He played with the tufts of hair at the side of his head. 'She *must* take the Reading–Newbury road. I wonder why he emphasised that "must"? He sounded very tense, too, very tense.'

Suddenly, he reached for the telephone and snapped: 'Operator, get me Stratton, near Newbury, 85 – and hurry.'

He replaced the receiver and sat staring at the telephone, then suddenly pressed a bell. A sergeant came in, and Chatworth said: 'Ask Superintendent Abbot to come here at once, please.' As soon as the door closed he picked up the receiver again and asked whether he had to wait all day for the call to Stratton, and when he had finished harrying the operator, the door opened and Superintendent Abbot sidled into the office.

Abbot was a tall, austere-looking man who never seemed to open a door in normal fashion, but always pushed it slowly open and seemed to creep in. He was an efficient, painstaking officer with a good record, but because of his cold, unfriendly manner he was given most of the unpleasant jobs at the Yard, such as carrying news of reprimands; he was probably the least popular officer in the Force.

'Good afternoon, sir,' said Abbot.

'Oh, Abbot, sit down. I've just had a peculiar call from West. He wants Griselda Fayne to be taken under escort to Kelham's Newbury house, and he has specified the route she is to take. There was something odd about the way he talked, almost' – Chatworth hesitated, and then said with a flash of inspiration: 'almost as if he were acting under pressure.'

'That isn't like West, sir.'

'That's exactly the point,' said Chatworth. 'It wasn't a

bit like West. We know this man Alexander is at liberty, and he's not what we might call orthodox at all. We also know that he wants information from Griselda Fayne. I think – just a minute,' he broke off, for the telephone rang. 'Hello – thanks. Hello?' A woman's voice answered him. 'Is that Mr Kelham's residence? . . . I think a Mr Mark Lessing is there. Ask him to speak to me, please . . . my name is Chatworth.'

There was a long pause, before Mark came on the line; and Mark was in no very good humour.

'Did you have to ring through here?' he demanded. 'I think I'm getting something from Mrs K. and—'

'Is West there?' demanded Chatworth, abruptly.

'Why, no,' said Mark, surprised. 'He left an hour ago, he must be on the outskirts of London by now. He took Blair with him. Why, what's the trouble?'

'I don't quite know,' said Chatworth. 'Listen carefully, Lessing, there's a good fellow. Griselda Fayne, you know about her, might turn up in about an hour and a half. If West comes back before she arrives, ask him to ring me at once. Is that clear? Thank you, Lessing, thank you, you're being a great help. Goodbye!'

He rang off again, and looked at Abbot thoughtfully.

'*Most* peculiar, Abbot. Something happened to make West change his mind about coming back here after he left Kelham's house. That suggests that he met something or someone on the road, doesn't it? Have *two* cars got ready for a journey at once, will you, and go down in one yourself – have Griselda Fayne released and send your man Martin and another sergeant with her. You follow with one or two men, and perhaps you'd better travel armed. I don't like firearms, but we can't be too careful in this business. Before you leave, come and see me again, but don't be too long.' He nodded dismissal, and then followed Abbot out of the office and went along to Roger's room, where three inspectors were clearing up at the end of the afternoon's work. Eddie Day jumped to his feet, and greeted the Assistant Commissioner with a broad smile.

'Anything I can do for you, sir?'

'I don't know,' growled Chatworth. 'Has West had any reports in during the last hour or two?'

Day hurried to Roger's desk and took a number of buff-coloured envelopes out of the 'In' tray; there were several memos also. 'Here they are, sir!'

Most of the reports were routine ones to do with the Kelham case – fingerprints, odd information about the movements of people implicated, a detailed survey of Ethel Downy's work with the Kelham Financial Trust, more particulars of Griselda Fayne, going back to the time when her father was alive, and – as instructive as anything – reports which showed that young Kelham's reputation with women had been a very unpleasant one. There was also a statement that a Mrs Iris Lesley, whose husband had just returned from the Middle East, was known to be a close friend of Griselda's, and lived at Ealing.

The telephone on Roger's desk rang.

'Hallo, Chief Inspector Day speaking . . . No, Inspector West is not here, but I will take a message—'

'I'll take it,' said Chatworth.

Eddie looked aggrieved as the telephone was snatched out of his grasp, and he stood watching. The other CI's went out.

'Well, what is it?' said Chatworth.

An impersonal voice greeted him.

'I am speaking from the Maidenhead Police Station with a message as requested for Chief Inspector West. A small Morris car, 8 horse-power, passed through Maidenhead at half past one today, believed to be the car about which Inspector West was asking information. The car was later reported to be involved in an accident with a Hillman, number 2BX12, five miles on the Reading side of Newbury. Is any further information required, please?'

'Yes,' said Chatworth, 'what about passengers?'

'Both cars were deserted, sir. It is believed that the occupants were injured and taken for medical assistance, and efforts are being made to trace them. Can you give any information about the name and appearance of the occupants, please.'

'Yes,' said Chatworth, and then amended hastily: 'No, not yet. I'll telephone you later.' He replaced the receiver and looked intently at Eddie Day. 'Well, well! Day, what's the number of West's car?'

Eddie drew in a deep breath, gripped his hands, and then the number came from him explosively:

'2BX12, sir!'

'*Thank* you, Day! An admirable memory. *Thank* you!'

Chatworth bustled out of the office, leaving Eddie looking after him with a beatific expression on his plain face.

Chatworth found Abbot waiting for him in his own office, and beamed at him.

'Abbot, we're getting on! West has been involved in a car crash, but he didn't tell me anything about it. Not a word about it! Now there's no doubt that there's something very funny afoot. Cancel the car you were going down in. I'll drive you down.'

'Do you think it's wise to get personally involved—' began Abbot.

'I don't care whether it's wise or not,' said Chatworth. 'I'm coming!' He lifted the telephone, and said to the operator: 'Call my flat and tell my man to telephone Lady FitzGeorge that I will not be able to put in an appearance this evening, I have been detained.' He rang off, and rubbed his hands together gleefully. 'Cunning fellow, West! Not by as much as a word did he warn me, but I couldn't mistake it, I just couldn't mistake his warning. Abbot, I wouldn't be surprised if we get that fellow Alexander after this, and once we've got him we certainly won't let him go! Is Griselda Fayne ready?'

'She's already in the car, sir.'

'Good,' said Chatworth. 'We'll leave ten minutes after her, and catch up the other side of Staines. Tell her driver not to go too fast!'

CHAPTER TWENTY

The Clash With Alexander

MR ALEXANDER hummed to himself as he waited for a signal from the road. He was standing on the hillock overlooking the road, some two hundred yards away from the farm-house where Roger was detained. Alexander still looked tired, but he also looked as if a great weight had been lifted from his shoulders, and now and again his humming took on a lilting gaiety.

Several cars passed along the road in each direction, and then there was a lull. From the hedge two men rolled a heavy barrel, which they stood on end in the middle of the road, and into the top they stuck a red flag. One man stood on either side of the barrel, and when a car came along it stopped and the two men went forward. Alexander watched tensely until the car reversed into a gateway and then began to go back. It was not Griselda, but a driver who had been warned that the road ahead was blocked because of an accident, and who had been told the best way to make a detour. Exactly the same thing was happening farther along the road, to keep this particular stretch clear. It had already been done once, earlier in the afternoon; the road had been blocked until an AA scout had wanted to see the scene of the accident and had duly advised the police of the two cars. Now the AA scout was off duty and Alexander believed that he would get away with this second piece of effrontery.

A second car came in sight.

'Now I wonder,' said Alexander, aloud. 'A black saloon – that's black – two men and the girl – there she is!' As he uttered the last words he put binoculars to his eyes, and then took them away and clapped his hands resonantly. His hopes were vindicated, for the car was allowed to pass. A little farther along the road, at the bend which had been fatal to Roger, there would be a hold-up, and if things went well Griselda would be at the farm-house within a quarter of an hour.

Alexander hurried back to the house.

In the yard stood a gleaming dark blue Packard, ready for the next journey. It was pointing along a secondary road which led away from Newbury, and Alexander had no fear of being caught once he started off with Griselda.

He entered the farm-house, and went upstairs to the study.

'Now we won't be long!' he boomed to Roger, who looked round from the bureau. 'Cheer up, Inspector! As I have told you I am a man of my word. In less than a quarter of an hour you will be released.' He chuckled. 'If you watch from this window you will probably see Griselda Fayne in a very few minutes!'

He gave a mock salute, and went out, leaving the door ajar and the man still on guard outside it. Roger, his heart beating uncomfortably fast, went to the window and looked out. He saw the gleaming Packard and Alexander standing by it. He made a mental note of the number of the Packard, and he noticed other things. The car was dark blue, and it had a mascot on the radiator cap, a rearing horse. He could see a corner of the upholstery; it was dark red. One of the windows was cracked in the top left-hand corner.

Suddenly he heard a voice. He watched closely, and he saw two men and Griselda approaching the house. Griselda was walking steadily, and her shoulders were squared, but there was no doubt that she was frightened. On one side of her was a farm labourer, on the other was Mortimer Bellew, who looked a little nervous.

Alexander bounded towards them.

'Splendid, splendid!' he boomed. 'My dear, how delighted I am to see you! I have freed you from the miserable attentions of the police force, and I hope your gratitude is as profound as it should be! Bellew! Fetch the other car. Griselda, climb into the Packard — you see how comfortable I am going to make you!'

Griselda stood still, facing him squarely.

'Why have you done this?'

'My dear child, this is no time for irrelevant questions,' said Alexander. 'Get inside! Edwards! Lock the door on the Inspector, and come down at once!'

'The Inspector!' exclaimed Griselda.

Alexander laughed.

'Your *bête noire,* my child! No less a person than Inspector West was persuaded to assist me in this little ruse.' He looked up at the window, but Roger was invisible from the grounds. 'I shall keep my word, she shall not be hurt!' boomed Alexander. 'Griselda, *do* get in!'

The door was locked on Roger. It seemed pointless to climb from the window, for there was a sheer drop to the flagged yard below, and there were no window-sills or convenient drain-pipes. He watched Griselda climb into the car. Two men sat in the back with her and Mortimer Bellew climbed in next to Alexander. As the engine of the Packard started up, Roger heard another car engine, and a small dilapidated Austin came into sight. In a few seconds the Packard was halfway along the lane leading to the farm-house and Edwards, who had been on guard until a few minutes before, was getting into the second car. Other men joined him, and the Austin followed in the wake of the Packard. After what seemed a long time the two engines faded.

In desperation, Roger pushed the window up, and looked out. There was an outbuilding farther along the house, on to which he could drop quite easily from a window a few yards away. Then he glanced up, and saw that the guttering of the roof was almost within reach. He lost no more time, but climbed out cautiously. The window-sill was a narrow one, and it was difficult for him to keep his balance, but by gripping the window-frame until the last moment he managed to stand upright and to grip the guttering. He tested it, and it seemed solid. He got a grip with his other hand, and then began to pull himself up.

There was a sudden rending sound, and he dropped with

sickening speed, his legs dangling. His heart seemed to turn over. He pictured himself hitting the flagged courtyard, but he held on grimly – and his fall was stopped. He looked up, to see that the guttering had come away for no more than six inches, and he could get back into the room if necessary.

Then he saw that the piece of guttering which had come loose was several feet long. If it were fastened securely at the point where it still held to the edge of the roof, and could be eased downwards gently, he would be able to drop to the courtyard. He took his arm away from the wall. The guttering sagged a little farther, and then stopped. He put his foot against the wall and tugged with his hands. The guttering came farther down. He hung there for what seemed a long time, until suddenly the guttering sagged again, and he thought that it would come away altogether, but it still held fast near the roof and he was no more than three feet from the ground.

He let go, and kept his balance when he landed.

There was a graze at the side of his hand, which was bleeding freely, and a tear in his sleeve, but these were his only injuries. He stood quite still, looking towards the hillock and the road along which the car had gone. The hillock was the best place for him to go; from it he could see where the nearest house was, and from the house he might be able to telephone. He started off at a smart pace, but suddenly the quiet of the countryside was broken by a powerful voice:

'Stop, there! Stop!'

'Great Scott!' gasped Roger, and swung round. 'That's Chatworth!'

Then he saw Chatworth coming over the brow of the little ridge in the copse. Beside him was the tall figure of Abbot, and behind them came two other men, who ran forward as he turned to face them. They were close enough to recognize him, and he saw Chatworth's astonished face.

'West! Upon my soul, West!'

'Get a car! cried Roger. 'I – no, get back to the road.

Come on!' he cried, and took Chatworth's arm and swung him round. 'They haven't been gone five minutes, we might pick them up!'

'You go on,' said Chatworth, after a moment of trying to run over the uneven ground. 'You go on, West!' He was gasping for breath.

Roger gave him a quick description of the cars and then raced to Chatworth's Humber, confounding the delay inevitable while he turned it round.

Abbot and two others joined him. He caught a glimpse of Chatworth's bold head in the copse before he started off. It took less than five minutes to reach the cross-roads, and coming towards them was an AA scout on a noisy motorcycle combination. Roger drew up with a screech of brakes, and shouted:

'Have you seen a Packard?'

'A what?' The man stopped and cut off his engine.

'A Packard!'

'Not on this road, lately!'

'Thanks!' cried Roger, and swung round the bend and along the narrow road. The road twisted and turned and there were tall hedges on either side. Abbot sat tight-lipped, obviously nervous. Roger, seeing in this a chance to redeem himself, took wild risks but escaped disaster. Soon the road widened and the hedges were lower, giving him better visibility. He drove at over sixty miles an hour, scanning the undulating countryside ahead of him. The sun was shining, and he thought he saw it glistening on the roof of a car not more than two miles ahead. He went even faster, and Abbot grunted but did not protest. Roger thought that he was gaining, and then he saw something behind the glistening roof of the car; it was the dilapidated Austin.

'We'll make it!' he muttered.

They were on a rise, and the road wound about the country in front of them, making both the cars clearly visible. He did not think that Alexander would realize that he was being followed. When the two cars disappeared behind a leafy hedge, however, he slowed down for the first time since leaving the AA scout – and as he turned the corner, he saw the Austin pulled up across the road. It had been there for some minutes, for none of its occupants were in sight.

'Be careful!' exclaimed Abbot.

'We can make it,' Roger said, and snapped over his shoulder: 'Jump out, you two. There are three or four men from that car nearby.'

As he squeezed past the Austin, his wing scraped noisily and some paint came off. The two men opened the back door and immediately he was past the obstacle they jumped down. Roger, knowing that the Packard could have gained half a mile in that time, trod more heavily on the accelerator, and heard Abbot grunt again.

Then a halt sign warned him of a major road ahead.

He could hear the rumble of heavy traffic, and slowed down. A small convoy of army lorries passed, and every moment he lost irritated Roger, but he dared not take the chance of slipping across the road between the lorries.

'We've had it,' he said, bitterly, as he moved off again.

'No one could say that you didn't try,' said Abbot, with a faint smile. 'I haven't been so frightened for a long time!'

'Nor have I,' said Roger. 'But we've got to get the beggar. I suppose we'll be wiser to stop here, and hope that someone comes along. I—' He broke off, seeing something in the hedge. There the grass was long, and it nearly covered a ditch, but he had caught sight of something dark; it looked like a man's coat. He slammed on the brakes and then got out of the car and ran back towards the dark-looking object. Abbot joined him. As they drew nearer, the thing materialized into the back of a man, and they could see one hand lying limp on the grass.

'I'll get him up,' said Roger.

His heart was beating fast as he went down on his knees beside the man, whose head was tucked down in the ditch, and whose feet and legs were almost covered in the grass. He put a hand beneath his waist and lifted him carefully, but when he saw the back of his head, cracked in like an eggshell, he knew that there was no need for caution. That was not the only thing; he saw the bald head and, on the grass beneath it, a wig.

It was Mortimer Bellew.

CHAPTER TWENTY-ONE

Mr. Alexander
Is Wanted For Murder

'WELL,' SAID Roger, in a low voice, 'we've got him for murder, anyhow.'

'I don't understand you,' said Abbot.

'Bellew was in the car with Alexander. He must have been killed in the car. I'd give a lot to know why.'

The little bald-headed man was now lying on his back, with a handkerchief spread over his face. His flesh was still warm to the touch, and his face was unmarked: only the back of his head had suffered. Roger, looking down on him, knew that Griselda must have been in the car when he had been killed, and the thought made him feel bleak. In the distance, he saw two or three vehicles approaching. He and Abbot stopped them, but no one remembered seeing a Packard. A man in a milk van, who said that he knew the district thoroughly, told him that there were half a dozen by-roads along which a car could have gone.

Then another car pulled up, and Chatworth climbed out.

'No luck?' he asked.

'I'm afraid not, sir,' said Roger, and turned to the milk-man, who was standing by ready to be helpful. 'Where is the nearest telephone – can you tell me?'

'There's an AA box about a mile down the road,' said the milkman.

'Good,' said Roger. 'We'd better send out a call for the Packard.' He was feeling tired; reaction had set in. He had relied on catching Alexander to make amends for his own actions, and now remorse was gnawing at him again, and filled him with a deep sense of shame. Chatworth looked at him curiously, and then said:

'Yes, all right. I – upon my soul, what have you been doing to my car? Look at that wing!'

'I'm sorry, sir,' said Roger. 'I—'

'Oh all right, all right,' said Chatworth. He looked at the wing, scowling, and then climbed into the driving-seat. 'We'll be back in ten minutes or so, Abbot. Look after things.' He waited for Roger to get in beside him, and drove off carefully. 'You nearly managed it, West,' he said and glanced at Roger, who was looking straight in front of him.

'How much good does "nearly" do?' asked Roger, bitterly.

'Now come, man! There's no need to be so glum. You did a very fine piece of work, and we came within an ace of getting him. Cheer up!'

'A fine piece of work!' cried Roger. 'Why, I—'

'That telephone call was a masterpiece,' said Chatworth, and went on heartily: 'I knew there was something wrong when you came through, and I made sure that we wouldn't slip up through ignoring you! Was Alexander in earshot when you telephoned?'

'Yes,' said Roger. 'He—'

'Then it was masterly!' declared Chatworth. 'Now let's hear no more about it. Ah, there's the AA box. You'd better handle it – here's a key for the box.' He handed Roger a key taken from a ring, and sat at the wheel while Roger went to the telephone and telephoned the Winchester Police. He gave them a full description of the Packard, and ask them to make sure that all other near by stations were advised.

'That's all right,' said the inspector to whom he spoke. 'As a matter of fact, we had a call about it a little while ago. We'll keep a sharp look-out.'

'The men in the car are dangerous,' Roger said shortly. 'They're armed and they'll shoot if they're in trouble. Make sure everyone understands that, won't you?'

'It's like that, is it? All right, Inspector.'

Roger replaced the receiver and returned to the car. He could not bring himself to smile in response to Chatworth's broad beam. His lips felt stiff and his hands were unsteady. He climbed into the car, while Chatworth shrugged his shoulders and gave a long-suffering sigh. He reversed into a gateway, and then started back along the road.

The body of Mortimer Bellew was in the back of the other police car, and Chatworth gave the word for it to be taken to London. Abbot went with that car, for the stranded Austin was driven up. The men who had deserted it had not been found, for not far from the road there had been a thick wood with several tracks through it. The local police had been asked to help, and Roger carefully gave descriptions. It seemed an age before that was finished and the other two cars had gone ahead, leaving him alone with Chatworth.

'Well, what do you suggest now?' asked Chatworth.

'I think we'd better see how Lessing is getting on, sir,' said Roger. 'Do you mind if I drive?'

Chatworth stared at him for a long time, and then without a word he got out of his seat. Soon they were driving at a fast pace on the shortest road to Newbury. It was thirteen miles away, and Stratton two miles on the near side of it. They passed through the village itself, the first time Roger had done so. Soon afterwards they saw *Poplars,* with the tall trees making clear silhouettes against a cloudless sky, and waving gently. The house looked attractive; a scene alien to the violence and murder with which it was connected.

Outside the drive gates Mellor was waiting with another Yard man. Roger pulled up.

'Is everything all right?'

'Yes, sir, as far as we can see from here.'

'You'd have heard if there'd been any trouble,' said Roger, and drove on, aware that Mellor was staring at him, puzzled. His set face explained that; he looked and felt very different from his usual self. He was conscious of Chatworth's curious gaze, and as he pulled up outside the house, Chatworth said:

'Now, West, what *is* making you look like a dog who'd lost a bone?'

Roger drew in his breath.

'You've nothing at all with which to reproach yourself,' said Chatworth. 'On the contrary, it was a very good piece of work, I tell you.'

'I wish I thought so, sir,' said Roger. He kept his hand on the gear lever, and turned to face Chatworth squarely. 'The truth is that Alexander frightened me into persuading you to release Griselda Fayne.' He spoke in a low-pitched voice, and his face was very pale. 'He gave me the choice of that, or being shot out of hand. He made capital out of my wife and—'

'Did you think he meant any harm to Griselda Fayne?'

Roger said: 'I think I convinced myself she would not be harmed. But I didn't have any certain proof. I risked her neck to save mine.'

'Flagellate yourself, if you must,' said Chatworth, 'but don't expect me to help you. You can only square things now by getting Alexander before he *can* harm Griselda.' He clapped Roger on the shoulder and barked: 'Now, West, what was Lessing doing here?'

Roger told him briefly.

He was mildly surprised that no one in the house had shown any interest in the arrival of the car, but when Chatworth told him of his brief telephone conversation with Mark, he assumed that his friend was still closeted with Mrs Kelham, and that the staff saw no point in making inquiries. They had been sitting there for twenty minutes before they got out and went to the front door.

'I don't think we should tell Mrs Kelham the truth, at this juncture,' Roger said. 'I'd like to get in touch with her doctor, and if necessary have one of our men examine her, so that we can be sure she is as ill as Blair makes out. I think we ought to do that before we take any risks.'

'So do I,' said Chatworth.

The trim little maid opened the door, and greeted Roger with a pleasant smile. Mark, it appeared, was with Mrs Kelham. There had been no other visitors that afternoon or evening. She went upstairs to tell Mark, leaving Roger and Chatworth in the drawing-room. It was beautifully furnished, with fragile-looking Chippendale chairs and settees placed about the pale blue carpet. A gilt star-shaped Louis XVI clock was over the mantelpiece, ticking loudly. The walls were painted a pale maroon red and the effect was restful and attractive.

'You did say something about going through the place,' said Chatworth. 'Was that just to get permission to come down here?'

Roger smiled. 'Not quite as crude as that, sir! I intend to go through everything on the premises, but at the time I thought it would be better to get – Great Scott!'

'*Now* what's the matter?' demanded Chatworth.

'I've forgotten Blair!' exclaimed Roger. 'Until this moment I'd completely forgotten that he was with me in the car when I was held up!'

'Your memory needs sharpening,' said Chatworth, with a smile which robbed the words of any sting. 'He was behind the hedge; our fellows had found him when we came along. He's in Newbury hospital by now, having his arm set.'

'Oh,' said Roger. 'So it was broken.' He swallowed hard, then managed a weak smile. 'I shall soon have to apply for sick leave, sir! I'm not myself.'

'You'll do,' said Chatworth. 'Lessing is a long time, isn't he?'

At that moment Mark came in. He waved to Chatworth cheerfully.

'Hallo, sir. Hallo, Roger,' he said. 'Well, I've spent over an hour with the old lady, and she's the sweetest creature I've ever met. And she worships her husband. Odd how many people seem to worship him, and others seem to hate him, isn't it? I don't know whether I've got anything that's going to be helpful,' he added, 'but at least it will be interesting. According to Lynda Kelham, her husband exerts himself a great deal to protect Alexander, who is his evil genius.'

'West also discovered that,' said Chatworth, acidly.

'But he didn't discover why,' said Mark, sweetly. 'I have done so. Kelham is loyal to Alexander for a most praiseworthy reason. They're half-brothers.'

Roger stared at him in unfeigned astonishment, and Chatworth looked taken aback. Mark beamed about him, fully satisfied by the effect of his words, and went on:

'It's quite true. Apparently Alexander – his full name is Alexander Kenneth Kelham, but he changed it by deed poll some years ago – was always something of a black sheep. He came into the picture during the war, when Andrew Kelham was already making headway. She believes that he really exerts a powerful influence over her husband, but she doesn't know why. She says that it started three years ago – the influence, I mean – and that Kelham has been a very troubled man since then. Are we making progress?'

Roger spoke slowly, after a long pause.

'I think we are. Blair said a curious thing when I first interviewed him – to the effect that he knew nothing of Kelham's past. He gave me the impression that he thought Kelham was either being blackmailed or else otherwise influenced by something he had done before he began to make headway.'

'His wife would probably know about such a thing,' said Chatworth. 'We can't take this consideration of her health too far, you know. If she has any knowledge, she must be made to divulge it as quickly as possible.'

'I don't think she is likely to know anything,' said Mark, breezily. 'Certainly she knows nothing from his more remote past, because they have only been married for six years. Anthony Kelham was the only child of his first marriage. I have done fairly well, you see,' he added, 'and I think we can take it for granted that Kelham has been blackmailed for something he did in the past. It might help to explain a lot, mightn't it?'

'I suppose it might,' said Roger, slowly.

'It's certainly very well worth knowing,' said Chatworth. He looked out of the window, was silent for a few seconds, and then said: 'Well, we can't stay here all night. Are you going to look through the house, West?' He glanced at Mark, and added sarcastically: 'I suppose Mrs Kelham's health won't suffer if we take that step?'

'I doubt if she'd know anything about it,' said Mark. 'The only servant is the maid who answered the door, and she is virtually in control. She's just getting Mrs Kelham to bed,' he added, 'and told me she would be down in a quarter of an hour.'

'Then I think we'll make a search,' said Roger, briskly.

He made the decision because he felt that he must do something, and there was little he could do at Scotland Yard if he returned at once. Chatworth said that he would go to see the Chief Constable of Berkshire, whom he knew, and would come back for them later in the evening. It was then a little after six o'clock. He went off breezily, and Roger watched him drive away before he heard footsteps in the hall. He told the maid what he intended to do, and was surprised when she said:

'Mr Kelham told me that if the police called I was to give them all possible assistance, sir, but to ask them not to worry Mrs Kelham. I'm sure you won't do that, sir.'

'No,' said Roger. 'What's the name of her doctor, do you know?'

'Sir Randolph Merlin, sir. He comes to see her once a week from Harley Street.' She said 'Harley Street' with slight but definite emphasis.

'Thanks,' smiled Roger.

Merlin was a specialist with an unblemished reputation; if he vouched for Mrs Kelham's condition, there would be no question of going over his head. Roger decided to put the matter to the test immediately, and telephoned Merlin's Harley Street house. He was lucky in finding the specialist in, and a few minutes sufficed to reassure him; the woman was really ill.

He rang off, thoughtfully.

'I can't imagine that Kelham would keep anything here which might encourage us to stay in possession,' he said. 'I don't think we'll find much, Mark.'

'Nor do I – and we won't find anything if we don't start,' said Mark.

It was dark before they had finished, and the maid came to ask them if they would like supper before they left. They accepted gladly. They had found nothing of the slightest interest; the only room where they had spent much time was Kelham's study, and in that there had been very few business papers; the private ones were completely innocuous.

Chatworth called for them just after nine o'clock. He told them that he had arranged for the Newbury Police to make a thorough search of the farm-house, and confided that he did not expect to find much there. He had been in touch with Scotland Yard, and there were no new reports. Nor was there any news about the Packard, which appeared to have vanished completely. He had telephoned the hospital, to find that Blair was comfortable, but would be detained there for a day or two at least.

'You can drive back, West,' he said. 'I don't like night driving. As a matter of fact I think I'll have a nap in the back,' he added. 'If you two must talk, talk softly!'

Roger and Mark walked to Bell Street from Chatworth's flat. Although it was getting on for midnight, Roger saw a light in the front room, but was reassured when one of the men on duty reported that the afternoon had been uneventful. Janet, in fact, was dozing in an easy chair, but she woke up with a start when Roger entered the front room. None of them felt like talking for long so they went to bed, and Janet was soon asleep.

Roger lay awake for an hour or more, tossing restlessly. The confused incidents of the affair kept running through his mind.

The baby woke him up with its plaintive hungry cry. Janet was awake but looked tired. Roger told her to stay in bed and went downstairs to warm the baby's food, which had been made overnight. Mark was still asleep.

Roger saw a Yard man on the opposite side of the road when he drew the curtains in the front room, and another from the kitchen window. He wondered whether it were necessary to maintain such a close guard, and decided that he would feel safer if he did so until Alexander was finally caught.

If he were caught—

He took the bottle up, and began to dress while Janet sat up in bed and Scoopy pulled at the bottle as if he were afraid that at any moment he would lose it. Roger began to talk; it eased his mind to tell Janet exactly what had happened with Griselda, and he knew that she would understand how the danger to the girl obsessed him.

A ring at the front door bell made him break off, and Janet said that the postman usually knocked. The ringing disturbed Mark, who called out to ask if anyone were up. Roger called out reassuringly and hurried downstairs, but the bell rang again before he opened the door.

On the porch were a Yard man and a taxi-driver; in the road stood a taxi, with the door open.

'Hallo,' said Roger, looking at the Yard man. 'What's the trouble?'

'It's a queer business, sir, and I thought I ought to call you,' said the other, anxiously. 'The cabby was given this address. The lady seems to be asleep, though, and we can't wake her up.'

'Lady?' asked Roger and then exclaimed aloud and rushed down the garden path, with his dressing-gown billowing behind him. He reached the taxi – and stood quite still, for Griselda Fayne was leaning back in a corner, her eyes closed and her face very pale.

CHAPTER TWENTY-TWO

The Plight of Gresilda

THE TAXI-DRIVER helped him to get Griselda out of the corner, and Roger carried her in. She was a dead weight in his arms, and did not seem to be breathing, although as far as he could see there were no signs of injury. He carried her upstairs and put her on the bed which he had just left, then left her with Janet, having found with relief that her pulse was beating faintly. Downstairs, he telephoned for the nearest doctor, whom he knew slightly, and then he spoke to the taxi-driver.

The man's story was simple and straightforward.

At seven o'clock he had been coasting along Putney High Street on his way to the West End, when a man and woman walking along the street had hailed him. He described the man as a 'hefty-looking fellow'; the woman, of course, was Griselda. The man had got out at Chelsea Town Hall, given the Bell Street address and paid him with a couple of pound notes, telling him to keep the change. The taxi-driver thought it funny but, as far as he knew, there was nothing the matter with the other passenger, and he had been astonished when he had seen her asleep.

'Did you hear her speak when the man got out?' asked Roger.

'I can't say as 'ow I remembers it,' said the cabby, a middle-aged man who looked apprehensive. 'I didn't give it a thought, that's the truth. There wasn't no reason why I should, was there?'

'No, you've no need to worry,' said Roger. 'Have you still got the notes?'

'O' course I have.'

'Swop them for two of mine, will you?' said Roger, and the cabby agreed. He seemed anxious to be off, but before he went Roger took the name of his garage, put through a telephone call, and made sure that the man's credentials were in order. He warned him that he might be called to give evidence, and, as the fellow was going off and he was slipping the notes into an envelope, he saw the doctor come in at the front door.

'I not only want to know how she is and what's the matter with her,' said Roger, leading the way upstairs, 'but I want to get a statement from her as quickly as possible. I think she's been drugged, but I can't go any further than that.'

'I'll look after her,' said the doctor, and went into Janet's room where Griselda still lay with her eyes closed, and her cheeks ashy pale.

Roger and Mark went downstairs.

Roger called the Yard and then inquired for Superintendent Abbot – which remarkable officer always seemed to be on duty. 'It's West here,' said Roger. 'Miss Fayne is back at my house – and I think it's time we had the ports and airfields watched.'

'They are being watched,' said Abbot, coldly.

'Oh,' said Roger, feeling foolish. 'That's quick work. Is there any news in this morning?'

'None fresh,' said Abbot. 'How is the woman?'

Roger told him, promised to telephone again as soon as he had the doctor's report, and returned thoughtfully to the kitchen. Mark had made tea, and took a tray up. The doctor was coming out of the room.

'Like a cup?' asked Mark, hospitably.

'Er – no, thank you, I – well, perhaps I will,' said the doctor. He smoothed his hair as Mark led the way into the spare room. 'I can't make up my mind what she has been given,' he said. 'I've found the puncture—'

'A hypo, was it?' asked Roger.

'Yes, and judging from the slight inflammation, recently used ,' said the doctor. 'It is undoubtedly a narcotic. I don't think it will be serious, but she is in a very heavy sleep and it may be some hours before she comes round. I don't think I would advise any injection to try to bring her round before she comes out of the coma,' he added, 'but if you're worried I should get another opinion. There are a lot of new narcotic preparations,' he added, 'I can't keep pace with them. Quite the best London man on narcotics is Sir Randolph Merlin, of course, but then you probably know that as well as I do.'

Roger stared at him, unblinking. One moment he was filled with confusion and uncertainty, facing a bewildering number of pieces of a puzzle which made no composite picture; and then some of the pieces fell into place, and he saw what had been hidden before.

'Mrs Kelham's doctor!' exclaimed Mark.

'The quicker I see Merlin the better,' said Roger, taking up his tea quickly. He took too much at a gulp, and winced. 'By jingo, that was hot! It's all right, doctor,' he added with a smile, 'I haven't taken leave of my senses, and you've been a wonderful help. Mark, be a good fellow and telephone Merlin for me, and make sure that he doesn't leave his house until I've seen him. Oh, and give Abbot a call and tell him what we know so far, will you?'

'Yes,' said Mark. 'What about breakfast?'

'I'll get some later,' said Roger.

He was ten minutes later than he need have been, because Scoopy took hold of his tie and was so fascinated with it that he and Janet chuckled in delight, while the infant tugged at it.

He was at Harley Street a little after half past eight.

A manservant opened the door, and Roger was shown into a long, bare waiting-room, in which the main piece of furniture was a polished table running the whole length of the room, and stacked at both ends with glossy magazines. The manservant returned after a few minutes.

'Sir Randolph can see you now, sir.'

'Thanks,' said Roger.

The specialist, whom he had met before and who had often given evidence in drug cases, was a tall, white-haired man with a surprisingly rubicund face and a manner more in keeping with a Regency dandy than a twentieth-century physician. His morning coat and striped trousers were a perfect fit, and he had the grand manner. He waved Roger to a chair in his surgery, crossed his legs, and put one delicate, white hand on a glass-topped desk. He offered cigarettes, and put his own in a long, ivory holder, before he said:

'I am very glad to be able to be of further assistance to the police, my dear Inspector. You have only to command me. I am sure you realize that.'

Roger said: 'What drug does Mrs Kelham take, Sir Randolph?'

Had he been less intent, he would have been amused at the change in Merlin's expression. He knew that if he had gone about the questioning in a more formal way, Merlin might have fallen back on professional etiquette and either refused to answer, or else declared that he must have Kelham's authority before he even discussed his patient. Now his expression gave him away; he was undoubtedly treating Mrs Kelham for drugs.

He accepted the *fait accompli* gracefully.

'If I now deny that she has ever taken drugs, Inspector, you will probably accuse me of lying. She has not had a relapse, I hope.'

'I don't think so,' said Roger. 'I hope you won't make it difficult for me, a great deal depends on what I can learn from you.' He did not think that Merlin would tell him the name of the drug at this juncture, so he added: 'Have you been treating her for very long?'

'Some three years,' said Merlin. 'You know, Inspector, I will gladly give you all the information at my disposal, but I must have a word with her husband first. I believe that he has been hurt.'

'He has, but how did you know?'

'His secretary told me,' said Merlin. 'He telephoned me from Newbury the other evening, and also asked me to make sure that you did not worry Mrs Kelham too much. When he mentioned you by name, I knew that he had no need for his concern.'

Roger thought: 'So that's what Blair was up to when he

hurried away at *Poplars*.' He smiled, and said aloud:

'I think Kelham is well enough to answer questions, but I hope you will answer one or two first. Does the drug induce long periods of sleep amounting to a state of coma?'

'Some drugs do,' said Merlin, blandly.

'Is it self-administered?' asked Roger, bluntly.

'I have every reason to think so,' said Merlin, 'or I would have advised Mr Kelham to inform the police.'

'Your point!' said Roger, smiling, and calling on a little blarney. 'Now, sir, you are probably the greatest living specialist in narcotic drugs. There is a girl suffering from such a drug now, and she is asleep at my house. I'd be very glad if you will come along and see her, as an early diagnosis is extremely urgent. Will you?'

'It rather disturbs my programme for the morning,' said Merlin, looking at his watch. 'I can squeeze in a very short visit, perhaps, if you do not live too far from here.'

'I'm at Chelsea, and I've a taxi waiting,' said Roger.

Twenty-five minutes later, Sir Randolph Merlin came out of Griselda's room, and looked Roger squarely in the eye.

'I do not think there is the slightest need for alarm, but it may be days before she comes round. I think she has been given a strong injection of laudanum, so it is nothing very novel. I think she should have a nurse, and we may have to give her artificial feeding once or twice before she comes round.'

Roger said: 'Isn't there any hope of getting her to talk today?'

'I don't advise it,' said Merlin.

Roger looked disappointed, and under cover of that put another question calculated to take the specialist off his guard.

'Could it be the same drug that is used on Mrs Kelham?'

Merlin put his head on one side, and said with a smile:

'You are a very persistent young man! I will gladly give you more information when I have Mr Kelham's permission. You will find me at my surgery after eleven o'clock, and until just before one. May I take your taxi again?'

Roger laughed, and went with him to the door.

He had no doubt that it was the same drug, and his relief at the report was not greatly tempered by the fact that Griselda would be able to tell him nothing for several days. Kelham was well enough to be questioned, and the time had come to be heavy-handed with him if he were obdurate.

He did not go to Kelham's flat immediately, however, but went to Cannon Row, where Guy Bellew was being detained. Bellew was now thoroughly frightened. The sergeant in charge said that he refused to eat his food, and when Roger saw the man's unsteady hand, he felt more hopeful than ever; Bellew was in no condition to withstand a shock, and then sharp questioning. Roger spoke with deliberate cruelty:

'Well, Bellew, I've some news for you.'

'W-what is it—' asked the long-chinned man. 'I – I can't tell you anything, Inspector, I was led away by—'

'I know all about your being led away,' said Roger, gruffly. 'Your brother has been murdered by Alexander.'

'M-m-murdered!' stammered Bellew. 'B-by—'

'By Alexander,' said Roger, roughly. 'Perhaps you think that the man is worth defending now.'

Bellew said: 'I – I hate the man! I've always hated him! He – he tried to make me kill Kelham. I refused, so he sent me with Newman. I was driven to it, I tell you, I was driven to it! I—'

Then Bellew broke off, and stared at Roger's back; for it had dawned upon Roger with devastating force that on Alexander's orders Mortimer Bellew had attacked Kelham and left him for dead, but that Alexander now knew that he was alive.

CHAPTER TWENTY-THREE

The Park Lane Flat

IN THE passage outside Kelham's flat a maid, with her back towards him, was running a noisy vacuum cleaner over the carpet. There were no other people about. He hurried past her, and rang the bell at the front door, his heart thumping unpleasantly.

Gardener opened the door.

'Why, hallo, sir,' he said, beaming. 'I wondered when you would look us up again.'

'Did you?' asked Roger, drawing a breath of relief. He went in, and Gardener eyed him affectionately. 'How are things?' asked Roger.

'Oh, perfectly all right, sir,' said Gardener. 'I take turns with Sergeant Wills, and we have at least one other man on duty all day. The nurse comes in every few hours, but there isn't much the matter with Mr Kelham, he'll be as right as ninepence in a few days!'

'Good!' said Roger. 'Do you know the nurse?'

'Oh, yes, sir. She's often done work for us, there's no need to worry about her. I give you my word,' went on Gardener, earnestly. 'I won't slip up again, sir. No one crosses the threshold unless we know them in person. There was a man here not long ago, and he really got mad when I wouldn't admit him. I did think of following him, sir, but that would have meant leaving Kelham, and I thought I'd better not.' Gardener smiled, reminiscently. 'He looked a bit of a bounder to me, sir, and talked rather like Alexander – you know, in the same rather flamboyant way. Oh, it *wasn't* Alexander,' went on Gardener with a grin. 'I wouldn't make any mistake about that, you needn't worry! He said he was a doctor. He wasn't the regular doctor, and so I just said I was sorry, and—'

Roger said: 'Did he give his name?'

'No,' said Gardener.

'Was he tall, well dressed, with white hair and a very red face?'

'Well I'm jiggered!' said Gardner, 'that's him to a T!'

'Then his name was Sir Randolph Merlin,' said Roger, with a faint smile, 'and I don't think he will be very pleased with you for refusing him admission!' He laughed at Gardener's obvious dismay. 'Don't worry, you couldn't have been expected to recognize him, and he should have given his name. If he comes again, you can admit him – but neither he nor anyone else may be left alone with Mr Kelham. That's an order.'

'I'll see to it,' said Gardener.

'Mind you do. I think I'll have a word with Mr Kelham,' went on Roger, and stepped towards the bedroom, the door of which was closed.

He tapped and entered on Kelham's 'Come in.'

Kelham was sitting up in bed, with a breakfast-tray at his side. His head was swathed in bandages, and only one eye was visible, but there were no scars on his cheeks or chin, and he smiled when he recognized Roger, and motioned to a chair.

'Come in, Inspector! I wondered when you were going to favour me with another visit! And I want to thank you,' he added as Roger sat down, 'for letting me come back here. It is much better than a nursing home or hospital, and your men serve a double purpose – they prevent newspaper representatives from bothering me.'

'I'm glad they're making themselves useful,' said Roger.

'They are very considerate,' said Kelham. 'Of course I know that on the pretext of guarding me they are really detaining me on your behalf, but just at the moment I am too tired to worry much about that. In fact I am anxious only about my wife. Blair should have come to tell me how she is by now.'

'Blair had an accident and broke his arm,' said Roger. 'He's not seriously hurt, but he's in hospital. Mrs. Kelham is quite well, however. I saw her only yesterday afternoon.'

'I see,' said Kelham. 'You are taking further advantage of my incapacitation to make a thorough job, Inspector! I have only one regret,' he added, good-humouredly, 'and that is that you won't be perfectly frank with me. I have told you that I am extremely anxious to help in every way I can, and I must admit that I find it a little trying to be suspected of the murder of my own son!'

'You are suspected of no such thing,' said Roger, 'but all necessary inquiries have to be made.' He knew that Kelham was probing, trying to find out the real reason for his interest, and he did not propose to give anything away. 'There is a matter about which I do want your help, though.'

'Name it,' said Kelham.

'Sir Randolph Merlin is naturally reluctant to tell me what drug your wife—'

He broke off, for Kelham's whole expression altered. He sat upright, his hands clenched, his lips set tightly, and the anger in his one visible eye was remarkably like that which Alexander had shown. For the first time there was a likeness between the half-brothers.

'She is simply ill!' snapped Kelham. 'There is no question of a drug!'

'Oh,' said Roger, thoughtfully. 'I'm sorry you feel like that about it. No one need know, apart from the police, and I shall have to find out somehow. If Merlin tells me, that will save me the need for arranging for other doctors to examine Mrs Kelham. I thought you would prefer that.'

Kelham said: 'I tell you that she is not drugged!'

'Unfortunately, I know that she is,' said Roger.

As he stared at the man, the whine of the vacuum cleaner sounded from the hall. It startled him, and made Kelham look towards the door. The man was still worked up, and his hands were clenching and unclenching. At that moment Roger felt that he was very near the truth; he did not think that Kelham would break down easily, but he was quite sure that he knew that his wife was suffering from some form of drug poisoning, and that it was connected with the mystery which surrounded him.

'Can't you stop that noise?' snapped Kelham. 'Every morning that blasted din is in my ears. Tell them to stop it!'

'It won't last long,' demurred Roger.

'Stop it, I tell you!' Kelham shouted.

He had gone to pieces very suddenly, and Roger shrugged his shoulders, stood up and went to the door. The vacuum cleaner was being run along the carpet near it, and the door banged against the machine. He could not make himself heard above the noise so he tapped the maid on the shoulder.

She switched off, and turned round.

Before Roger recognized her, before he dreamed of the truth, she kicked him viciously in the pit of the stomach. He saw it coming and just managed to evade the full force of the kick, but it sent him off his balance, and she rushed past him into the bedroom. Gardener, sitting by the wall, jumped up in alarm, but Roger recovered before the maid reached the door, and swung round.

The maid was Ethel Downy!

From her white dress she had snatched a gun; he could see it in her hand as she rushed at Kelham, who drew back in the bed, his face blanched. It all happened very swiftly; the woman had not yet levelled the gun, and Roger leapt desperately towards her, snatching at a chair as he went. He pushed the chair along the carpet. It touched the back of her legs, and made her lose her balance as she fired. The roar of the shot was deafening. The bullet passed Kelham's face and buried itself in the wall, and before Roger could stop her, the woman had swung round and levelled the gun at him.

He flung himself forward.

He felt the wind of the bullet as he closed with her. He gripped her right wrist and twisted it so that she screamed with pain, and the automatic dropped to the carpet. She was not beaten even then, but tried to get herself free and struck and kicked wildly at him. Her fingers clawed his face, and he felt a sharp pain as one nail touched the tip of his nose, re-opening the wound. Then Gardener passed him, and boxed her ears so soundly that she swayed from side to side, all the fight knocked out of her.

'The little vixen!' said Gardener, in a restrained voice.

'Nicely done,' said Roger. 'Handcuff her.' He watched Gardener fasten handcuffs on her wrists, and then looked at her coldly. 'That was one of your mistakes,' he said. 'Did Alexander send you?'

She said: 'Supposing he did?'

'I'll deal with you later,' said Roger, and turned to Kelham, who was white-faced and trembling. 'The bullet didn't touch you, did it?' he asked.

'No, I'm all right,' said Kelham. 'But your nose—'

'It's only a scratch,' said Roger, dabbing his nose, which was now bleeding freely, with a handkerchief. 'Not more than I deserve. Nice exhibition of brotherly love, isn't it?'

Kelham caught his breath. 'What – what are you talking about?'

'Your half-brother's emissary,' said Roger. 'Isn't it time you stopped being obstructive? Isn't it time you stopped pretending to be helpful, but actually keeping back the only information of importance? You've lied twice this morning. You know that your wife is suffering from a narcotic drug and you also know that Alexander is your half-brother. Whatever thing is keeping you silent, whatever ugly skeleton there is in your cupboard, we'll find it sooner or later. It will be much better if we get the information in a voluntary statement, instead of having to find out by delving deeper and deeper into your past. None of us likes muck-raking. I wish—'

He broke off, for Gardener, who had taken Ethel Downy into the outer room, tapped on the door, and said:

'Inspector, Dr Merlin – I mean Sir Randolph Merlin has come again. He wants to see you.'

Roger said: 'Show him in, and then take the woman to

Cannon Row.' He looked at Kelham, and added quietly: 'This may be your only chance of making a full statement and cooperating. Take it.'

Merlin came in on the words.

If he were annoyed at his earlier rebuff, he hid it successfully, smiled at Roger and put his hat, stick and gloves in a chair. Then he advanced towards Kelham, rubbing his hands together softly.

'Well, Andy, here I am at last! How are you, old fellow?' Merlin in such a bluff mood was a new experience for Roger, and he was surprised that the men were on such familiar terms.

'There is nothing much the matter with me,' said Kelham. 'Be quiet a minute, Randolph.' He sat quite still, closing his eyes, and Merlin looked reproachfully at Roger, who ignored him and stared at the injured financier. The silence lasted for what seemed a long time. He imagined something of the inner battle going on in Kelham, and he hoped that Merlin would do nothing to interfere.

At last, Kelham opened his eyes.

'All right, West,' he said, hesitantly. 'Randolph, don't interrupt.' He paused again, and then went on in a firmer voice: 'I have been victimized by my half-brother, Alexander, for some years. I have been blackmailed, tormented, and forced into courses of action which were against my own wishes and my own principles. There were two causes for this blackmail. In the first place, I have gained some eminence in the financial world. I could not have done so if it were generally known that—'

'Andy!' exclaimed Merlin. 'There is no need—'

'It had better all come out,' said Kelham. 'Be a good fellow and don't interrupt. I was going to say, West, that it would have been impossible for me to reach my present position had it been generally known that I served a three-year sentence for embezzlement – not here, but in America.'

Roger said nothing; he was not wholly surprised, for it had become very clear that the past had an important bearing on the present; but the fact that the crime had been in America, and had been paid for with three years in jail, was unexpected.

'I had made the legal restitution for my sins,' said Kelham, 'and I will make no attempt to gloss over the fact – I did embezzle my client's money, although, like everyone who does so, I thought I would be able to replace it before it was found out. That episode in my past would, of course, have prevented me from adopting a financial career in England. I did not think that it was known over here. I had used a different name when in America, and posed as an American citizen. I made what we know as a fresh start in England' – there was a wealth of irony in his voice – 'and was making considerable progress when my half-brother came and saw me. Alexander was never a particularly honest man, but has always been brilliantly clever. Both of us have a peculiar faculty, that of completely mastering finance. The difference between us is, I think, that he is amoral, whereas I now try to act up to a code of behaviour which is generally accepted as honest. However, I need not waste words in whitewashing myself.'

He paused again, and groped for cigarettes on the table by his side. In doing so he nearly knocked over one of the plates on the tray. Roger gave him a cigarette, and lit it.

'Thank you,' said Kelham. 'I knew that Alexander would try to coerce me into certain courses of action which I would dislike. To try to stop him, I financed him and allowed him to go his own way. I thought that I had succeeded until I made the discovery – through Merlin, here – that my wife's poor health was due to a narcotic drug, a form of laudanum. I thought that she was suffering from a sleeping sickness, but Merlin quickly disabused me. It was clear from the start that the drug was being administered cunningly. To this day I do not know how it was done, and is being done. I only know that I sent her to *Poplars*, I surrounded her with servants whom I believed to be trustworthy, and I tried to make sure that no one inimical to her would have access to the house. No matter what precautions I took, however, the drug still reached her. There would be periods when she was on the mend, and then she would suffer a sharp relapse. I did all I could to find out who was giving her the drug, but I failed completely. I knew *who* was arranging it – Alexander. But he had a stranglehold on me, and continually strengthened it. I could only have stopped him by telling the truth about my past. And I would have done that, even at the risk of losing everything, had that been the only thing at stake. But he drugged my wife, and made it clear that the process would go on whether he were free or not. I believed him. Merlin was able to assure me that the drug would not prove fatal in the quantities with which she was being treated. So I was under his thumb. You know that I was involved in doubtful schemes, and now you know why. The next step was an obvious one. I saw the possibilities in the land boom. My interests were mainly financial of course, and I tried to keep from Alexander the fact that I was acquiring several large estates at a fair price. I was also acquiring interests in firms of building contractors, in brickfields, and in allied industries. I naturally wanted as much influence as I could get. I tell you, West, that it was my sincere intention to make homes at a reasonable price for the working people of this country. I was satisfied with moderate profits. I knew that there would be a great deal of speculation, and I hoped, with Government assistance, to check them. However, Alexander found out. He sold me some land, through a nominee, which had forged conveyances. He bribed a town council employee, in my name, to give him information about land to be taken over for Council development, bought the land cheap and sold it at a big profit. He made it look as if I were trying to corner the market for illegal profit-taking. He made Government departments suspicious of my intentions. His method was simple. I was to make big profits, some illegally – and he would blackmail me for a share of those profits. I couldn't prove he had committed the crimes, but he could fake proof that I had. I know all this sounds incredible,' Kelham added, wearily, 'but it is the truth. Apart from the blackmail, I had to do as he wished, or else see my wife die before my eyes. Every time she suffered a relapse it was like a dagger pointing at my heart. I knew, of course, that Alexander would soon make bigger demands on me. He had carefully prepared the stage, and sooner or later he would demand my full cooperation. He had his own plans prepared, you see – plans for taking control of some of the larger firms in the allied building trades, in which I already had a large interest.

'Alexander is very wealthy. He had no difficulty in getting men to work for him, for he pays extremely well. He might be described as a pirate, a buccaneer determined to take fat prizes from whichever victim seemed the most easily attacked. By the time the war ended and there was an opportunity for beginning the rebuilding programme, he had contrived to make himself extremely powerful. Using my name – you might say that I served as a guinea pig – he waxed more and more powerful. I was charged with negotiating with the Ministry of Works, and all the time the threat to my wife increased.

'I have no doubt that I aroused the suspicions of the police,' went on Kelham. 'In fact I know that I did, and I know why your attitude has been so hostile, Inspector – not openly so, but enough for me to see. That was but one aspect. I also made enemies. I did not know at first that some small firms in which I bought interests were reduced almost to ruin by Alexander, so that they could be bought cheaply. Charles Blair's father was the owner of one of them, and he killed himself. Griselda Fayne's father was another; he tried to kill himself, and as the affairs of his business were in great disorder and he had broken the criminal law, he was sent to Broadmoor. Charles Blair came to see me, but I was able to persuade him that I had done all I could to help. He became the most loyal servant I have ever had. Griselda did not tell me openly that she knew. I love the child,' he added, very gently. 'There is something very beautiful about Griselda. I hoped that I would break down her hostility. I even hoped that she would marry my son, and that there would be peace between us. Unfortunately, she knew that Anthony, for all his excellent qualities, was unreliable when women were around.

And there was a time when he got out of hand, was drunk most nights, and became a positive savage. On one such night he and Griselda had their bitterest quarrel, but I did not give up hope even then, I kept on trying. You see, Inspector?'

'Yes,' said Roger, quietly.

'There were many trivial results of the unholy partnership,' went on Kelham, bitterly. 'Other people who thought I had wronged them wrote me threatening letters, and I ignored them. I had so many at one time that I would not even see them, and told Charles to destroy them all. I kept on, hoping and praying that the day would come when I would discover how it was that Alexander managed to continue to get the drugs to my wife. It was an obsession. I determined that I would work with him just as long as there was danger to her. I may have been wrong, but that was my decision. Even when Anthony was murdered, I kept to my course. I do not know who killed him. Sometimes I think that it was Alexander, and that perhaps Anthony had discovered his true nature. At others, I think that he was killed by someone who believed he or she had good reason to hate me, and mistook him for me – we were very much alike. Of course, I knew that there was a risk that you would find out there was much more happening than there appeared on the surface, but I was determined at all costs to try to save my wife. I wonder whether you would have discovered my half-brother's part in this if he had not been foolish enough to come to your house and to try to get Griselda away.'

'Sooner or later it would have come out,' said Roger. 'Do you know why he was so anxious to get Griselda?'

He tried to make the question sound casual, but he knew that much depended on it. He waited, while Kelham seemed to be trying to frame an answer, and then the man said, quietly:

'Where is Griselda now?'

'At my house, being well cared for,' said Roger. 'I—'

'Griselda, of course! I heard the name mentioned at your house!' exclaimed Merlin, and Kelham started. 'Andy, the child is suffering from *exactly* the same drug as Lynda!'

Kelham drew in his breath, and eyed Roger coldly.

'So you let her go,' he said, and the words turned the sword in Roger's wound. 'You let the beast get her.'

Roger said: 'She will not be in danger now, and we can also protect your wife. You must tell me, if you know, why Alexander was so desperately anxious to see her.'

'I am not sure,' said Kelham, 'but I think it was because she knows who killed Anthony.'

CHAPTER TWENTY-FOUR

Fingerprints of Great Interest

IF KELHAM's theory was the right one, there were puzzling features which preoccupied Roger as he returned to Scotland Yard. He had spent another two minutes talking to Kelham, and a few of the points which the man had made had been elaborated. The larger problem was solved, but it was a curiously unsatisfactory solution. While Alexander remained free, he would be dangerous. It was clear that he had worked not only behind his half-brother, but also behind other people whom Roger did not know. Kelham believed that he had established a powerful syndicate in which his nominees had great influence in all building and allied trades, and that, without once revealing himself, Alexander would take great profits. It had seemed to Kelham that for some time his half-brother had believed that the stages of preparation were all but completed; that was borne out by Alexander's great confidence in his own future.

Roger telephoned Chatworth, and was told to go to his office immediately. He marshalled his thoughts as he went upstairs, and told Chatworth everything he had learned.

The AC seemed fascinated by the story, and when Roger had finished, he pulled at the tufts of hair at his temples until they stuck out at right angles, and said heartily:

'That's a very fine report, West, a very fine report. You must have handled Kelham extremely well! Now all we want is Alexander.'

'All!' exclaimed Roger.

'Oh, we'll get him,' said Chatworth. 'What about this Downy girl? Has she talked?'

'I haven't tried to make her, yet,' said Roger, 'I thought it would be better to keep her on edge for a few hours.'

He saw Guy Bellew before he interrogated Ethel Downy. Bellew was now in a mood to make a full confession. It proved that he had worked with Alexander on the wrong side of the law for some time; so had his brother and Newman. Gradually Alexander had forced them into a position where they had to obey him, or be betrayed to the police. They had always known, too, that he might choose to murder them; Mr Alexander was a past-master in the art of blackmail.

'And I haven't the faintest notion of where to find him!' Roger muttered as he went from Bellew's cell to Ethel Downy's. 'For once I almost wish I weren't a policeman – I'd make the little vixen talk then!' The limitations of police regulations had never been more irksome.

Ethel Downy did not refuse to talk; she simply said that her parents had been ruined by Kelham and that she had tried to kill him because of that, and she had helped Alexander because he was an enemy of Kelham's.

'When did you start helping Alexander?' Roger demanded.

'Years ago,' she said. 'He discovered that I hated Kelham, and it's no use asking me how, I don't know. I would have helped anyone who wanted to harm Kelham.' Her voice was spiteful, and it seemed to Roger that she believed her hatred to be well founded. '*You* people wouldn't do anything, so—'

Roger interrupted sharply: 'What do you mean by that?'

'I kept writing to you,' muttered Ethel Downy.

'I see,' said Roger, slowly, knowing that another part of the puzzle was solved. 'You used Griselda Fayne's type-writer to write to Kelham and to the police, did you?'

'Supposing I did! I never had any time for Griselda, the stuck-up little beast. I knew she was a friend of Kelham's, so she deserved what she got.'

Roger made no comment. The girl said that she knew nothing of Alexander's hiding places, and professed to know little of what he did. She was pert and, to Roger's surprise, she seemed confident that she was in no great danger. He spent an hour talking to her, and came away with no more useful information, still dogged by the nag-ging realization that Alexander, somewhere in England, was laughing at him.

He went home to lunch, and was glad to find Mark there. For once he paid only the slightest attention to Scoopy who was gurgling in his pram, and discoursed at some length; when he had finished, Mark said thought-fully:

'So there are just two questions – where is Alexander? and who killed Anthony Kelham?'

'I'm in a frame of mind where I don't much care who killed Anthony Kelham,' said Roger. 'All I want is to arrest Alexander. I've been on the telephone to all the places where he might be hiding-out – I mean, all police head-quarters within a hundred miles of Newbury, and there hasn't been a sign of him. Confound it, that Packard couldn't have been spirited away!'

'Hasn't it been seen *any*where?' asked Janet.

'She isn't very bright today,' said Mark, apologetically. 'Scoopy and tummy-ache this morning, and it's distracted her. Hang it, Roger, the car must have gone to earth some-where.'

Roger put his head on one side.

'Who did you say isn't very bright?'

'Have any of those men who ran away from the Austin

you talked about been found?' asked Janet.

'Yes,' said Roger. 'They were found hiding in a copse. The Winchester police got them, eventually. I was on the telephone about it just before I came home. They all say that they had no idea where Alexander was going, and that he had instructed them to follow his car. He didn't intend that too many people should know where to find him,' he added, bitterly. 'Oh, we've got a lot of the well-paid crooks, and one or two of them will probably be charged with conspiracy to murder, but—' he shrugged his shoulders. 'They don't really matter. Alexander's our man. I've got a damnable feeling that we'll never see him again,' he added. 'I think I've been troubled at the thought that Alexander would defeat us, right from the first. His confidence was almost unnerving. The very fact that he let me go free, and sent Griselda back, is a measure of his confidence.' He lit a cigarette gloomily, and broke a match on his bread plate.

'Handsome West in the doldrums,' said Mark. 'I wonder why there was an earnest desire, at one time, to kill you?'

'I probably imagined it,' said Roger. 'Alexander might have been playing on my nerves, to get me in the right frame of mind for delivering up Griselda.'

'Now that's nonsense,' said Mark. 'Newman was waiting to kill you at the Ealing house. By the way, what about that friend of Griselda's, and the possibly vengeful husband? Have you been to see her?'

'If he was so anxious to kill you,' Janet said, practically, 'why did he let you go?'

'That's the crux of the question,' said Roger. 'There must be an answer to it, but it's just as puzzling as why he let Griselda go. The fact that he has drugged and put her to sleep for what might be two or three days makes one thing evident,' he added. 'He wants a short time to complete his preparations.' He stubbed out his cigarette, and pushed his chair back. 'We'll get the beggar!' he added, and looked more cheerful than he had done during the meal.

'I suppose there's nothing I can do,' said Mark.

'I don't see that there is, at the moment,' said Roger. 'If there's anything at all, I'll telephone you.'

'I suppose,' repeated Mark, with apparent innocence, 'the use of a car wouldn't persuade you to let me drive you about?'

'Come on!' said Roger, laughing.

Mark got it out of the garage, and soon they were driving towards Scotland Yard. The same problems faced Roger, the same thoughts kept passing through his mind, and all the time the one urgent problem was to catch Alexander. He had rarely felt so utterly at a loss.

Coming out of the Yard was the police-surgeon, with a black brief-case swinging in his hand as he hurried down the steps. He pulled up when he saw Roger.

'West, I've just seen Sloan.'

'How is he?' asked Roger, quickly.

'Out of danger,' said the doctor, and went on his way.

The news cheered Roger up a little, and before he reached his office there was another item, more significant, although unlikely to yield immediate results. The Packard had been found abandoned in a wood near Guildford.

'It looks as if they were heading for London,' said Roger, as he and Mark walked towards his office. 'It'll be an hour or two before we get any more information about that, though.'

In the office Eddie Day was sitting at his desk, and spoke as soon as Roger opened the door.

'I say, Handsome, Parky wants to see you, he says it's urgent. Why, if it isn't Mr Lessing. How are you Mr Lessing?' Eddie shuffled to his feet and advanced to shake hands, and then detained Mark in trivial conversation while Roger went upstairs to the fingerprint office.

It was a poky little place, with one wall filled with a large window to get the best light. A small bench was crowded with oddments, many of them covered with a greyish-white dust on which the marks of fingerprints showed up clearly. Inspector Parker, the Yard's fingerprint expert, looked up and grinned.

'I thought that would fetch you,' he said, 'I told Eddie Day that I would have his blood if he didn't tell you the moment you came in. I think I've got something for you.'

'I need it badly enough,' said Roger, ruefully.

'Come along with me,' said Parker. He led the way to another, much larger office, where the walls were fitted with shelves on which reposed hundreds of thousands of fingerprints, carefully filed away. Roger had never really got used to the amazing system by which it was possible for Parker and his numerous helpers to find particular fingerprints at a few minutes' notice.

'Here we are,' said Parker. 'There was a set of prints at Kelham's flat which I couldn't identify at first, and then I had a brainwave and looked through the letters.' He picked up a foolscap sheet, on which were marked the prints of thumb and four fingers of both hands; all of them were small, and Roger thought they were a woman's. 'There weren't many at Kelham's flat,' said Parker, 'but we got one good set, you see. Now – look at that.'

He opened a cardboard file of papers, marked at a foolscap sheet, and Roger saw an identical set of prints. The loops and whorls were well defined, and he knew there was not the slightest doubt that they belonged to the same person.

'Mrs Millicent Garner,' said Parker, with a broad smile, 'who went down for three years for running a brothel and some other nasty business a few years back. Ever seen her before?' he added, and from the file he slipped a large head-and-shoulder photograph.

Roger gasped: 'Great Scott! The matron of the hostel!'

'Now known as Agatha Barton,' said Parker, with great satisfaction. 'I knew it was the same woman when I saw one of the photographs you brought back from that hostel, Handsome. Not bad, eh?'

'Not bad!' exclaimed Roger. 'It's a miracle!' He stood staring at Parker's florid face, his mind working at lightning speed. 'So the hostel's matron visited Kelham's flat, she's in this business. What a complete fool I've been! When the false message was telephoned to the cinema, it was from somewhere with a private telephone exchange, yet when I saw one at the hostel I didn't give it a second thought! Parky, I'm in your debt for life!'

'I'll remind you of that,' said Parker, as Roger hurried out and went to his own office.

Mark and Eddie Day stared when he rushed to the telephone and banged the receiver up and down, then asked for Chatworth. A moment later he said:

'West here, sir. I'd like authority to raid the hostel in Buckingham Palace Gate in some strength – may I go ahead? The woman Barton is known to have been at Kelham's flat, probably on the day of the murder ... Yes, I'll see to it, sir, thanks!' He rang off, and looked jubilantly at Mark. 'Now we're moving! Eddie, be a hero and ask Abbot to arrange for eight men, will you, I've got another call to make.'

'That's all very well—' began Eddie, and then he sighed and lifted the receiver, for Roger was already asking for Kelham's flat. Gardener answered him, as bright as ever, and in a few seconds he was speaking to Andrew Kelham.

He said: 'It's West here. Kelham, do you own the hostel where Griselda Fayne lived?'

'No,' said Kelham. 'But my half-brother owns several houses along there.'

'Do you know the woman who runs it?'

'I don't think so,' said Kelham. 'Just a moment, West.' He was silent for some seconds, and then went on: 'I've been trying to think where I could find out exactly what property Alexander owns there, but I'm not really sure. You'll find it in the Bellews' records, I think, they sold it to him.'

'Thanks,' said Roger, and asked: 'Let me have a word with my man, will you? Thanks ... Gardener, listen to me. Don't allow Mr Kelham to use the telephone, nor to go out, but report immediately to me here if he tries to do one or the other.'

'Very good, sir,' said Gardener, cautiously. 'That will be all right, sir, I'm not a bit tired.'

Roger grinned at the elaborate way in which the man prevented Kelham from guessing the topic of conversation. He rang off and hurried to the door, telling Mark that he would be back in a quarter of an hour. He hurried along the passages and down the steps, and, to the astonishment of the policemen on duty, he ran across the courtyard, out of the gates, and into Cannon Row. He called out to the sergeant on duty, say: 'I want to see Bellew, at once.'

'Okay, sir.' The man swung his keys and began to walk leisurely along the cells.

'Hurry!' cried Roger, and the sergeant broke into a trot.

Guy Bellew was huddled up on a hard wooden chair. He looked up when the key grated in the lock, but did not try to get to his feet. He looked so utterly dejected that, in spite of his own elation, Roger felt sorry for him.

'Bellew, this might make a lot of difference to your future. Tell me at once what property Alexander owns in Buckingham Palace Gate. I know he owns the hostel, at 21B. What others are there?'

Bellew made no effort to be evasive.

'He owns three, with the hostel in the middle,' he said. 'We sold them to him years ago.'

'No others?' asked Roger.

'Not as far as I know,' said Bellew. 'What do you mean, it might make a lot of difference, Inspector?'

'It means that I'll do all I can for you,' said Roger. 'All right, sergeant, that's all.'

He turned and hurried out of the police station. As he turned into the Yard gates, he saw two police cars outside the front entrance, and men were already getting into them. Mark was standing by his Lancia.

'Ready?' he asked, eagerly.

'All ready,' said Roger. 'Come on.'

CHAPTER TWENTY-FIVE

A Raid in Force

'I DON'T like being a Jonah,' said Mark Lessing, 'but you seem to be taking it for granted that you'll find Alexander at the hostel. It's not really likely that he got into London again, and even if he did he'll know that that place is likely to be suspect.'

'Not he,' said Roger, confidently. 'Why should it be? He even tied up Agatha Barton, and used Ethel Downy to make it look as if he had no influence at the place. That's the reason for his confidence, and his one big mistake. We'll find him there.'

'I hope you're right,' said Mark.

Roger grinned, and yet the cautious attitude made him thoughtful. It was the last place where he would have thought of looking but for Parker's perspicacity, and he thought that Alexander would feel quite secure there. Yet it was obviously possible that the man was somewhere in the country. Even if he were, however, the matron would probably know something about his movements.

He sent one car, with four men, to the back of the house where they were reinforced by the man on duty there, and left the other four outside, with strict instructions to watch the adjoining houses, also reinforced by the man on duty. Then he and Mark approached the front door of the hostel and knocked loudly.

The maid whom he had seen before opened the door.

'Good afternoon,' she said.

'Hallo,' said Roger. 'Is Mrs Barton in?'

'*Miss* Barton, sir,' said the girl. 'Yes, she's in her office. I'll tell her—'

'Don't worry,' said Roger. 'Go along to the kitchen, and tell the cook that you've both got to be out of the house within two minutes. Don't worry about clothes, just get out. You'll see some men at the back, and they'll look after you. Hurry, now!'

The girl gasped; but she turned and hurried to the kitchen while Roger walked along the passage to the office door. It opened as he reached it, and 'Miss Barton' stood on the threshold, staring at him unpleasantly.

'Really!' she said. 'You might at least have the courtesy to send word that—'

'Not again, Mrs Garner,' said Roger, 'the time for politeness is past.'

She backed away from him, her hands clenched at her breast and her face ashen. She tried to speak, but although her lips quivered, she could not utter a word, and she knocked against her desk and fell.

'Where is Alexander?' demanded Roger.

She licked her lips, and croaked: 'Who – who do you mean?'

'Alexander is the fat man for whom you work,' said Roger. 'Did he also use a different name? Where is he?'

She gasped: 'I – I don't know what you mean. I—'

'Start thinking very hard,' said Roger.

Then he saw that her hand was groping behind her for the telephone switchboard. He let her grope, speaking all the time, until she touched a switch – and then he pounced, and dragged her away; the switch was not touched. Mark stepped forward swiftly, and took her other arm.

'So you'd try to warn him, would you?' said Roger. 'Listen to me, Garner. I intend to know where Alexander is within the next five minutes. You may have a chance to turn Queen's Evidence, but you'll lose that chance if you're obstinate now.'

'I – I don't know anything! You've made a dreadful mistake, a dreadful mistake!' Her voice was high-pitched, and she was gasping for breath. 'I don't know any Alexander. I tell you I don't know—'

Roger snapped: 'You were at Kelham's flat on the night his son was murdered. I have evidence that you fired the bullet which killed him. Alexander gave me the evidence.'

She cried: 'That's a lie!'

'Lie or not, I've a warrant for your arrest,' said Roger, making a play of taking a paper out of his pocket. 'He wasn't so loyal to you, you see.' He drew out the warrant for the search of the hostel. 'Millicent Garner, *alias* Agatha Barton, I—'

'He's in the cellar!' she cried. 'It runs under three houses!'

Then, suddenly, she groaned and fell forward in a dead faint.

Roger said: 'Not bad, Mark. Stay here a moment, will you?' He went to the front door and beckoned his men. 'Three of you come with me,' he said. 'Two of you watch all three doors, and if anyone tries to get out and won't stop, shoot to wound.' To one of the men who came in with him, he said: 'Go and give the same instructions to the men at the back. Three of them are to come back with you.'

'Right, sir!'

'Now for the cellar door,' said Roger.

'Don't take it too carelessly,' warned Mark, 'he might be able to overhear anything said up here.'

'I know,' said Roger. He walked along the passage to the kitchen, and stopped by a door beneath the stairs. It was locked. He began to pick it, but even when the lock was clicked back – as his men arrived and crowded in the passage – the door would not open.

'Bolted,' said Roger. 'Two strong men – forward!'

All the men laughed and moved forward in a body.

'Two, I said,' said Roger. 'Parrish, you and Fraser can do it, and don't forget we want it down in a hurry.'

The two most powerful men of the party launched themselves against the door. The thought passed through Roger's mind that they might find it impossible to break down, for Alexander might have reinforced it with steel; it might even be electrically controlled. He went so far as to wonder gloomily whether he should have brought a man with an oxy-acetylene burner along; but then the two stalwarts put their weight against the door, and on the third

lunge the bolts on the door gave way, and they were pre-
cipitated through the entrance. There was a small landing
immediately in front of them, and they came up against
it.

'All right,' said Roger. 'Mark, stay here!'

He pushed forward, but Mark, disobeying him, was the
next to start down the stairs. Roger went with his gun at
the ready. One of the men at the top had switched on a
light, which filled the staircase and the little square lobby
below with a bright glare. Their footsteps were muffled on
thick carpet, and the floor of the lobby was similarly
covered.

Ahead of them was another closed door.

'Strong men forward again,' called Roger softly.

He was pressing himself against the wall to let the others
pass when the door opened from the inside. He saw it in
time, and covered the opening with his automatic. He
caught a glimpse of Alexander's face – and then the door
was slammed again.

Before the bolts could be pushed home the two hefties
had launched themselves against it. They went through at
the first attempt, and Roger pushed past them into another
lighted room, where Alexander was squeezing through
another doorway. He was facing them, and he held a
gun.

Roger and Alexander fired at the same moment, but the
fat man's bullet went wide, and Roger scored a hit on his
forearm. Alexander winced, and tried to squeeze through
the doorway, but it was not wide enough, and he was
jammed so tightly that Roger was able to catch up with
him and grip his sound arm. He pulled the man forward
savagely. Alexander lurched towards him, holding up his
injured arm, and gasping for breath.

'Watch for others!' Roger snapped.

Mark and three men hurried through the doorway,
while Roger and Alexander stood facing each other.
Elation surged through Roger. In the fat man's eyes there
was still a hint of bewilderment, as if this were the last
thing he had expected, and that even now he could hardly

believe that it had happened. Roger waited, feeling a sense of anti-climax. Now that it was over and he had his men, he realized what a shambles it might have been if Alexander had prepared to defend himself to the last; one sub-machine gun or automatic rifle would have caused terrible execution.

'Well,' he said, after a long pause. 'That's put paid to your account, Alexander. I want you for murder.'

Alexander opened his little mouth, and in a piping voice he said:

'I did not kill young Kelham!'

'I think you did,' said Roger, 'and I know you killed Mortimer Bellew.'

Alexander squeaked: 'He – he tried to get out of the car, he fell out—'

'And after killing himself, hid in a ditch,' said Roger sarcastically. 'There isn't any hope for you. You're through.'

Alexander said: 'West, West, listen to me. I gave *you* a chance! I was going to write to you to tell you my half-brother killed young Kelham, and what other devilry he's up to. You don't know what a mistake you're making. I've only tried to prevent him from doing his devilish work, that's all! I'll tell you everything, *every*thing, if you'll give me a chance, the same as I gave you. And I let Griselda Fayne come back, I didn't hurt her, she'll be all right in a day or two—'

'Kelham has told me everything,' said Roger, 'and I don't propose to treat you lightly.'

'He's a congenital liar! Give me a chance, West, just one chance. I – I couldn't help it, I had to do it. I tell you that you want Andrew, not me. He's really arranged it all! West' – he stretched out his sound arm, beseechingly. 'Don't be hard, West. I beg you not to be hard. I have been inspired by the highest motives, I beg you to believe that. Have I done *you* any harm? Have I ever done more than frighten you? Have I—'

'You're wasting time,' said Roger. 'And Newman did more than frighten me.'

He saw Mark coming through the doorway with the other policemen and three men whom he recognized as some of those who had been at the farm-house; they were now safely handcuffed. It was a complete victory, yet in spite of his scepticism, Alexander had succeeded in making him less confident that he had heard all the truth from Kelham. True, that was insignificant compared with the change in the fat man. His voice remained thin and piping and his lips were twitching; he was obviously frightened. Roger thought that he was staring at him, really hoping that he would relent. He was wary, all the same, in case the man tried to wreak vengeance before the final disaster overcame him.

'I – I always told you Newman worked for someone else besides me,' said Alexander. 'He worked for my half-brother. Why don't you believe me, West, instead of standing and staring at me as if I were something horrible? Listen to me! You will be doing a grave injustice if you do not release me and arrest Andrew. *He* is to blame. Doubtless he has pitched a fine story to you, has hidden behind me, hoping to make me suffer for *his* sins. It is not right, West, it is not right!'

Roger frowned, and seemed to relax. Alexander's eyes widened, there was a look of hope in them, and Mark, who came back to join them, stared in bewilderment at Roger, who said:

'Look here, Alexander, supposing I *can* help you? I'm not interested in getting my own back, I want the murderer of Anthony Kelham. No policeman who's got his wits about him interferes with big business!'

'West, I knew you were a gentleman, I have always known it! Be reasonable, my friend, be helpful, and I will make it well worth your while.'

'If only I knew why you wanted Griselda, and what was in those papers you talked about,' Roger said, doubtfully, while Mark looked up at the ceiling, amazed that Alexander was being taken in by this apparent indecisiveness.

'That is simple, West! Naturally I did not want you to find me here, I knew that Andrew would malign me. I thought that perhaps Griselda knew that I sometimes stayed here, and I had to find out. Those papers were sent to her in error by the Bellews. They contained the agreement by which I bought these three houses. You see how vital it was for me to find out whether she had read them. She had, West, and she thought it would help her if she kept silent. So I sent her to sleep. I intended to be here only for a short while, and she could not have known that I intended to leave the country, nor where I went. She told me, also, that the papers were tucked into a pocket of the typewriter desk, that is why you did not find them. Ethel Downy eventually found them. I once thought you had read them, otherwise I would not have sent Newman to—'

'Kill me. So that's it,' said Roger, and he felt as if a great load had been lifted from his mind. Alexander's statement explained so much about Griselda and her importance; and the only question remaining was to find the name of the murderer of Anthony Kelham. 'All right, Alexander, I will put in a word for you if I can. Who killed young Kelham and Mrs Ricketts?' He hoped his promise would elicit more information.

'I did not! I swear I did not!'

'I'm not interested in who didn't,' said Roger. 'Was it the woman upstairs – Garner or Barton?'

'I don't think so. She swears that she did not know who killed him, although she was in the flat at the time. She saw Griselda and heard the quarrel. After Griselda had gone a man came in and shot him, and then went away. Agatha hurried out by the back stairs quickly; she was frightened, terribly frightened.'

'Why was she there?' asked Roger.

'I had sent her there. I had a key and gave it to her. I knew that Griselda was going to see Anthony, and wished to know what the conversation was about, but I do not think Agatha fired that fatal shot. Griselda was troubled about some letters written by a friend, that is all I know. I was most anxious to know what Anthony would say. I wanted to make sure that he would not betray me, that—'

Roger snapped: 'So he worked for you?'

'He – he performed one or two little services for me, that is all,' said Alexander, retracting hastily. 'He was a nice lad. I was very fond of him.'

'He was a young scoundrel,' said Roger, and added harshly: 'Did *he* poison his step-mother? Is that how you evaded Kelham's watchfulness?'

'Why – why, what a remarkable idea! I did no such thing, I assure you. Poison his step-mother, indeed! I—'

'We're just wasting time,' said Roger, abruptly. 'We'd better get along to the Yard.'

'No, West, no!' Alexander screamed; he still seemed to think that Roger might let him go, and Roger had difficulty in keeping his disgust and his astonishment out of his expression. 'I beg you to give me a chance,' gasped Alexander, pawing at his arm. 'I will admit it, I did administer gentle drugs to Lynda, and Anthony did give them to her, in the form of chocolates and in her drinks. He did it in return for a substantial allowance from me. His father kept him very short of money, not approving of his loose living, and Anthony had to have more. I – West!' Alexander drew back, and raised his hand to his chin. 'West, do you think that Andrew discovered that fact? Do you think—'

'Never mind what I think!' said Roger, roughly, and he turned and called to the man in the doorway. 'Take him to Scotland Yard, and don't handle him gently if he tries to get away.'

He waited until the fat man, gasping for breath and still sending imploring glances towards him, had left the cellar, before he looked at Mark, who said:

'So Kelham killed his son?'

'Because the son was administering drugs to his step-mother,' said Roger. 'I think so. The difficulty will be to break his alibi.'

'Do you want to break it?' asked Mark, quietly.

CHAPTER TWENTY-SIX

The Alibi

ROGER ADMITTED that he did not want to break the alibi, but he had no choice. He believed that Kelham had told him the truth; he believed that the man had killed his own son when he had discovered the devilry of which he was capable. He believed that Alexander was everything that Kelham said, and that it would soon be proved.

First, he had to make sure whether Kelham could have killed his son.

He returned to the Yard after Alexander was safely lodged at Cannon Row and made his report to Chatworth, leaving the theory of the murder until the last. Chatworth looked startled, and his immediate comment was the obvious one.

'Didn't you tell me that Kelham and Blair had perfectly sound alibis for the evening in question?'

'According to various reports, they had,' said Roger. 'Here they are, sir.' He opened a manila folder, and read from them. 'At four-thirty, in conference with three directors of the Kelham Financial Trust. The meeting lasted until five-thirty, which would let Kelham out. Each of the directors was questioned, each corroborated the statement. That may mean, of course, that they were deliberately protecting Kelham. I don't think we will do much good interrogating them again yet, sir. I'm more likely to get the information from Blair.'

'How can you do that? He is fiercely loyal to Kelham.'

'Will you leave it to me, sir?' asked Roger.

'Hum,' said Chatworth. 'Hum. Yes, all right.'

Roger invited Mark to drive him to Newbury, and Mark, seeing his friend's face set, said little on the journey. He drove fast, and as Roger saw the pleasant countryside flash by, and drew nearer to the little town, all the things that had happened passed through his mind. He thought of Scoopy; and of the probability that at one time Kelham had thought as much of his son as any man. He tried to imagine the terrible pitch to which circumstances had brought Kelham, even driving him to kill his own son.

'Shall I come up with you?' asked Mark, when they reached the hospital where Blair was in a private ward.

'Yes,' said Roger.

Blair was lying back and reading. The ward was bright and sunny, and he looked less harassed than Roger had yet seen him. He looked up with a smile, which faded when he saw Roger's expression; he put his book down, and hoisted himself up on his pillows. He seemed very young.

'Well, West?' he said.

'I have a nasty job to do,' said Roger. 'I have to arrest a person on a charge of murder, which will almost certainly be proved, but I do not believe it is the right person. I can't help myself. The evidence is there, the case is watertight. There is no alternative.'

Blair said: 'I see. I didn't kill Tony Kelham.'

'I don't for a moment think you did. I don't intend to charge you.' Roger smiled. 'I am going straight back to London, to charge Griselda.'

Blair stiffened. 'You can't do that! She didn't kill him!'

'She was present,' said Roger. 'She had a motive. She had tried to kill him before. The only way to save her from being hanged is to find the real murderer. My superiors are satisfied that we have found her. As far as they are concerned, the case is closed. I've a soft spot for Griselda—'

Blair said, in an agonized voice:

'Stop, West, Stop! *I* killed Tony!'

There was a short, tense pause. The confession was so unexpected that Roger gaped, and yet he was suddenly convinced that it was the truth.

'I was away from the directors' meeting for twenty minutes,' Blair went on. 'I drove to the flat, went in and shot him, and then drove back. I threw the gun into some bushes in Hyde Park.' He closed his eyes, and added in a voice little above a whisper: 'I knew how anguished Andy was about his wife's illness, and I found laudanum in Tony's room one day – I suspected him, and searched for the poison. If Andy ever learned the truth, I knew it would break him. I already hated Tony Kelham, because of Griselda, because he was a young devil, because he wasn't fit to live, but most of all I hated him because of the torment he caused to Andy. I did it deliberately, and I would gladly do it again.'

He stopped, and there was silence in the room. In Roger's ears the blood was throbbing. He had not dreamed of this; but now he had no doubt that it was true. Here was a man who loved Andrew Kelham as few men had ever loved another. In his confession there was an explanation for all that remained unsolved. The great tragedy was that at his trial the truth would be known; he could not save Kelham from learning of his son's real beastliness.

Then Mark snapped: 'Look out, Roger!'

Suddenly, Blair flung back the bedclothes and leapt towards the window, which was ajar. He pushed it wider open and vaulted to the sill, but before he could jump to his death, Roger had reached him, and they pulled him back into the room. There were tears in his eyes, and he was saying:

'Let me kill myself, there needn't be a trial then. Spare Andy the trial, West, spare him the trial.'

Roger said: 'There are times when I do not like being a policeman. I'm sorry, Blair, but you'll have to see it through.'

One evening in September, Roger walked slowly home from Scotland Yard, hardly noticing the passers-by, and often bumping into them. In his mind's eye there was a picture of the scene at the Old Bailey that afternoon, the third day of the trial of Charles Blair for Anthony Kelham's murder. Alexander and his accomplices had already been tried and found guilty of Mrs Ricketts's murder, of which the Bellews had been accessories before and after the fact, and Alexander himself had been convicted of Mortimer Bellew's murder.

Everything had been made clear at the earlier trials.

On the night of Anthony Kelham's death, Agatha Barton had been to the Park Lane flat and seen the body. The woman Ricketts had also seen her. Newman had been prompt to make sure that the charwoman was silenced, taking the back-door key away to confuse the issue further.

Andrew Kelham had been in the witness-box several times, and there was no doubt that he had already told Roger the whole truth: he had obeyed his half-brother because of the danger in which his wife stood. In all Kelham's companies, Alexander had an interest, working through unscrupulous directors many of whom were being held on various charges. Alexander had hoped to force land and building prices up to a high level; Kelham's plan was to keep them down, but Alexander had been too strong for him. Directly Alexander had realized where police investigations would lead, he had put his half-brother on the spot, intending to kill him before he could be persuaded to tell the police the whole story.

Roger thought of Griselda, and how easy it would have been to make a case against her. He did not think she would ever carry a gun again. She had held a licence for many years, as pistol shooting had been her favourite hobby.

As he turned into the path the door opened and Janet hurried out. The baby was crying plaintively in his pram in the hall.

'What happened?' Janet demanded, tensely.

'Guilty, of course,' said Roger. 'When we found the gun in a flower-bed in Hyde Park, that was a foregone conclusion.' He put his arm about Janet's waist, and they went into the hall; on seeing them Scoopy stopped crying, and simply opened his mouth.

'Hungry, old chap?' asked Roger, smiling. 'Is Mummy starving 'oo?'

'He *is* late,' said Janet, 'I couldn't settle to anything.

Griselda was here until four o'clock, and then she went out and wouldn't say where she was going, Roger, I—' she broke off, and her eyes filled with tears. 'Pick him up,' she said in a choked voice, and hurried to the kitchen.

Roger lifted the baby, who gurgled and pulled his hair, and then went thoughtfully into the sitting-room. When Janet came in, ten minutes later, he was bouncing Scoopy up and down on his knees, but his smile was mechanical. As soon as she took the child, he went to the telephone and dialled a number. Janet watched him, the bottle hovering about Scoopy's mouth, until his crying made her realize what she was doing.

'Hallo,' said Roger. 'Hallo – is that Mr Andrew Kelham's flat?'

'Yes,' said a girl. 'Who is that?'

'Inspector West,' said Roger. 'I – hallo! Is that you Griselda?' He shot an amazed glance at Janet. 'Is it?'

'Yes,' said Griselda, 'yes, I had to come to see if I could help, I feel such a beast. I'll fetch him in a minute, he'll be glad you've called. But' – she hesitated, and then added quickly: 'Will they hang Charles, Roger?'

'I think he has a good chance of being reprieved,' Roger said. 'Try to be patient, Griselda.'

He thought he heard her sob, and there followed a long pause before he heard Kelham's steady voice.

'Hallo, West. This is very thoughtful of you.'

'Not at all,' said Roger. The words sounded inane. 'How – how is Mrs Kelham?'

'Practically fit again,' said Kelham. 'We shall go to live at Newbury, and Griselda has agreed to come and live with us in our retirement.' There was no bitterness in his voice, but he sounded anxious when he went on: 'Don't feel sorry for me, West. About Charles now – did you mean what you said to Griselda?'

'Yes, I meant it.'

'If you get a chance, West, will you tell him that – that Griselda—' He broke off.

'I'll tell him,' said Roger, very gently.

TRAVIS McGEE

JOHN D. MACDONALD

The tough, amoral and action crammed
stories of the popular Travis McGee as
he tangles with passionate women and
violent men to uncover blackmail and
corruption from California to Mexico.

**First of the Travis McGee series
now filming starring Rod Taylor.**

All available at (20p) 4/- each

THE QUICK RED FOX
A DEADLY SHADE OF GOLD
BRIGHT ORANGE FOR THE SHROUD
THE DEEP BLUE GOODBYE
NIGHTMARE IN PINK
A PURPLE PLACE FOR DYING